I0683016

The World of Carnival

Gladys Swan

Serving House Books

The World of Carnival

Copyright © 2009 Gladys Swan

Cover painting: "Finale" by Gladys Swan

Author photo by Lou Faber

Serving House Books logo by Barry Lereng Wilmont

ISBN: 978-0-9825462-3-9

Published by Serving House Books

www.servinghousebooks.com

First Edition 2009

Second Edition 2018

Contents

Acknowledgments

"Carnival for the Gods" appeared originally in *Sewanee Review* and in book form in the novel *Carnival for the Gods* (Vintage Contemporaries, 1986).

"Small Wonder" was a published finalist in *Best New Writing 2008*.

"The Dream of Circus" was published originally in *Sewanee Review* and was awarded that magazine's Tate Poetry Prize in 2001.

Gladys Swan has published five novels, *Carnival for the Gods*, (Vintage Contemporaries Series), *Ghost Dance: A Play of Voices*, (LSU Press, nominated for the PEN/ Faulkner Award), *A Dark Gamble*, *Ancestors*, and *Small Wonder*, as well as seven collections of short fiction. Her short fiction has appeared in such literary magazines as the *Kenyon Review*, *Sewanee Review*, *Virginia Quarterly Review*, *Shenandoah*, *Manoa*, *Ohio Review*, and *Prairie Schooner*, where she was awarded the Lawrence Foundation Prize for Fiction.

In 2001, she received the Tate Prize for Poetry from the *Sewanee Review*. She was awarded one of the first Open Fellowships from the Lilly Endowment for a study of Inuit art and mythology and has held residencies at Yaddo, the Fundacion Valpariso in Spain, the Chateau de Lavigny in Switzerland, and the Martha's Vineyard Writers' Residency. She has received various fellowships for residencies in painting at the Vermont Studio Center, where she has also been a Guest Writer. An exhibit of her paintings, together with her poetry, was held in the Fall of 2004 at Stephens College in Columbia, Missouri. She has done the cover art for several literary magazines and books, including her own. The cover art for this one is a painting entitled "Finale."

Introductory Note

In this chapbook, you will find the first chapters of *Carnival for the Gods*, and the four novels that form a sequence from Gladys Swan's comic fantasy, first published in the Vintage Contemporaries Series. *The World of Carnival* continues with its original inhabitants and their struggles against the odds: Alta and Dusty, who dream big; the midget Curran, who undertakes a journey at the behest of the acrobat Elise, whose son has gone mad (*Small Wonder*); Amazing Grace, whose talents as a performer bring gasps from her audience and lead her to the challenge of creating herself (*Dancing with Snakes*); the Kid, who, after a long search, sets out to find the Seventh City, picking up along the way a melancholy Jew, who grew up there (*The Dream Seekers*). And, finally, a return to Alta, who finds herself drawn back to the circus to follow another set of dreams (*Down to Earth*). The series of novels explores the relations between life and art, reality and illusion, the openness to possibility and the capacity for the renewal of energies within a culture. It is the writer's major work, and it is her dream that the sequence may one day be published.

Spirit Over Water: Gladys Swan's World

Ein begriffener Gott ist kein Gott. A God comprehended is no God.
Rudolf Otto

"Back of the curtains, what is there to see?"
"The Dream of Circus," poem by Gladys Swan

Terror has its sublimity, the sublime, its terrors. Or as Rilke wrote: every angel is terrifying. When one thinks of courageous writers, one often thinks of those intrepid souls like Mandelstam or Ritsos who challenged existing regimes and were imprisoned, gulaged, or disappeared. Gladys Swan is a courageous writer of another sort, alive in an age and culture in which writers who dare are not imprisoned but ignored. Swan's bravery as an artist reveals itself in her unflinching scrutiny of humankind's shadow, her works, maps of recovery to our lost selves. As Carl Jung defined the shadow, it is that part of our psyche, hidden from consciousness, that is the repository of aspects of ourselves we deem shameful, unworthy, evil, improper, bad. Gladys Swan's charge to her readers is that we take this inner life lightly at our peril.

Swan allows us to experience a character's struggle with the unredeemed and discarded parts. If ignored or misused, the shadow can turn explosively dangerous, projected onto scapegoats and the "alien" others we fear and hate. And yet through the tribulation of facing this repressed energy tremendous creativity is released. The mysterious voice in the desert, the nightmares, the peach tree that shines forth beckon and elude. Swan implies the divine, hiding out in our shadows, cannot be understood via language or rational thought, but must be experienced. This experience of the depths, what theologian Rudolf Otto called

"The Holy," is, contrarily ominous and numinous, awesome and awful. There is usually a moment in a Gladys Swan story when a character is confronted by the holy, the *Mysterium Tremendum*. It happens to Mrs. Grenebaum gazing at her peach tree in winter, to Rachel on the last pages of "Gate of Ivory, Gate of Horn." Curran, the midget in Carnival for the Gods, lost in a strange garden among evocatively disturbing statues thinks: "It was dark and he wanted to get out. Not just dark, but foul. Everything touched some secret vulnerability, threatened him with contagion. Who had worshipped here?"

Contact with the numinous causes us to shudder and turn away. Swan suggests we must go deeper into the territory. Instances of the formerly blind acquiring insight abound in Gladys Swan's fiction, which itself bears a visionary, mystical cast. In her tour de force novel *Carnival for the Gods*, poised to become a classic, Alta, her husband Dusty, the midget Curran, the giant Donovan, Billy Bigelow, Amazing Grace and the boy head out in search of a new paradise, and the soul-restoration they did not know they needed. The given visions do not necessarily heal, nor are they comforting, but perhaps that is Swan's point: we cannot know the consequences of our seeking, only that we will be changed by it.

Numinous consciousness adheres to any number of Gladys Swan's characters, some of whom have no understanding of their capability. Nonetheless, in what might be considered acts of grace, certain characters attain visionary experiences that alter their lives. In an early story, "The Tiger's Eye" Walter Lawrence, a disaffected fellow and a thief of his neighbor's roses, strikes up a friendship with the tiger at the local zoo. Via dialogues with the beast, Lawrence recognizes the existential dilemmas of his own life—confinement, stagnation, moldering resentment, apathy, extreme loneliness—mirrored in the life of the caged tiger. Further, his recognition results not from a projection of the human onto the animal, but from empathy by way of the imagination, which allows for the heart to open to the suffering of another species. All that society condemns—passion, brutality, extreme beauty, fearlessness—lodges itself in the form of the tiger, and it is the imprisonment of those values, shamed and despised by society, that is suffered by man and beast.

8

Of Memory and Desire; News From the Volcano; Carnival For the Gods; Ghost Dance: A Play of Voices; On the Edge of the Desert; A Garden Amid Fires—the titles of Gladys Swan's books throw an illuminating beam on her concerns. Freaks, drifters, disgruntled isolates, and outsiders of all breeds inhabit her pages. They are precisely the ones—unaffiliated to an ideology and incurious about psychology—who are emblematic of a culture bereft of a defining myth. Unsure what is happening to them, these characters are besieged by dreams or strange events and can only scratch their heads over their existence.

Naturally the conditions of knowledge are tragicomic, the pratfalls many, the stakes, life or death of the soul. One might say Swan has an activist's imagination, though she engages us at the suprapolitcial level beyond the concerns of governance by nation-state. Her activism takes the form of a moral imperative that propels her characters to investigate what lies beneath cruelty, falsehood, desire, pride. Swan exhibits sensitivity to the poignant yearnings of her characters, yearnings that are often incomprehensible to the yearners. As readers, we recognize them as our own. How could we not? They are the universal longings of all sentient beings across millennia and constitute the force behind our search for meaning through a compassionate relationship to our kind and to the natural world. It is Swan's gift to remind us that the quest for a spiritual life is neither a lofty notion confined to clergy, New Agers, or an educated populace. Quite the contrary, any of us, at any time, maybe prodded, provoked, stricken, pushed out of our homes, and unwittingly dragged, dazed by circumstances, onto the path of self-knowledge. We are, at some level, all incarnated as fools, or like the Fool of the tarot deck, we start the journey in ignorance and innocence, our head in the clouds, our few provisions in a knapsack over our shoulder, the instinctual life, our loyal guide, represented by the dog at our heels. What we encounter on the path and how we respond is our unique story.

If the attainment of self-knowledge is a personal imperative, it is also, in Gladys Swan's world, a necessary ingredient for a community's evolvement. In "Spirit Over Water," a mother in despair over the conditions of her life, and the life of the turbulent whirlwind of her daughter Jade, thinks to herself: "And she [Jade] was through with politics: the faction and delay, the meanness and self-interest. Let all that go too. Let the past be cut away like a bloody fragment." But for Swan, it is precisely the past, its personal and the collective burden that cannot be cut away. For all the pestilence and corruption the past carries, Gladys Swan insists that a vision of rebirth and renewal for the individual and the culture is possible only when the past is faced and acknowledged. What drives one to take on this arduous and exhausting task? Above and beyond personal guilt, with its pricks of conscience and psychological necessity, humankind possesses a desire for beauty that rests on an expanded perception of the interconnectedness of all life, as suggested by the origins of the word atonement—"at-one-with."

We do not exist apart from the larger whole; our individual spiritual growth contributes directly to the wisdom of the collective. Swan illustrates that our reclamation of a personal past, our devotion to and release from anger, fear, revenge, and the cleansing aspects of loss and forgiveness, far from being solipsistic, are the antidote to a culture's travails. In the way of quantum theory, our private epiphanic awakenings reverberate throughout the stratosphere.

To read Gladys Swan is to be engaged in transformation. Experience and not analysis, the limbic system and not the late-developing frontal cortex, the five senses and not rational thought are the engine of change.

—Dale Kushner

Carnival for the Gods

It was the first time Dusty had ever backhanded her, and it was not just the blow, the pain, the blood from her lip flowing saltily into her mouth that gave Alta the shock: it was the sense that something fatal had struck at the roots of her life. Things would never be the same. It was the edge of Dusty's ring that had cut her lip, a gold ring with a strange little head carved in ivory that he'd bought during a fit of extravagance in Kansas City and said was his good luck and that he'd never part with it. As she stood in the cramped little bathroom, looking into the mirror, teeth all outlined in red as though she'd been eating red-hearted plums or pomegranates, the lip still bleeding, it seemed as though she'd never staunch the flow. This is my life, she thought; this is time leaking away, as it has been doing year upon year. And I'm standing here letting it happen like I was born without a brain.

The whole of the little trailer had shaken with their quarrel, till even words and the clash of voices could not contain the violence. Pansy, the little curly-haired dog she kept, a cross between a poodle and a wire-haired terrier, had taken refuge under the couch and, looking at Alta with brown eyes that seemed full of the light of tragedy, still refused to come out. Dusty meanwhile had thrown himself out of the trailer and into the truck, banging doors all the way, setting up a cloud of dust as he roared off into town, leaving her there alone with the freaks and the animals in the broken-down carnival. She dabbed at her lip as she tried to calm her feelings. She was looking pretty terrible at the moment. Face blotched, bags under her eyes, broken lip, but she wasn't all that old—forty-seven—and there was still a chance for ... what? For love, for money?

Money talks—she'd learned that much. It says yes and it says no. Says, you owe it to yourself, baby; go on and have it. Be my guest. Says, you're out of luck, sister. Says, go to the city and have yourself a ball;

says, stay home and starve your gut. Says, turn on the gold-plated faucet, break out the champagne. Says, stay away, lady, you smell bad, and nobody's gonna give you a second look. Says, dream—the sky's the limit. Says, look at the walls peeling. Says, go hang yourself.

It says, Alta concluded, you have been with a man who's brought you nothing but trouble and grief, all the while promising you the world. And where has it landed you? Down in the flatlands with blood on your teeth. Always full of harebrained schemes. And he wasn't half as crazy as the rest of the outfit, only more unreliable.

"I'm sick of this life. Filled up to here." That's how it had begun. Dusty, sitting at the narrow formica-topped table with the bench on either side, at which they had shared what might be called their domestic life, was adding up one of his interminable columns of figures. Always trying to turn nothing into something, as Alta had it, to make less come out to be more. "Sick of it." He looked up: "There's no anchor hanging out of your ass."

The truth of this observation left her momentarily speechless— a yawl in a dead wind. Then her fury unlidded, and the fine brew the years had whipped to froth came boiling over, pouring out: the salt was in her mouth, the distillation of years of sweat and tears and gall. All she might have had—all that had gone down the drain.

It was the sandstorm that finally did it to her. Bad enough to have the equipment truck break down in the flattest, most god-forsaken stretch of natural freakishness she'd ever laid eyes on. Like somebody's uninteresting nightmare. A world created out of what any sensible being would've rejected in the first place or else reached for only in the dry heaves of violent boredom: things twisted and sharp and spiny and hard. Some of them reached up and out with arms dried and dead in their attitudes of empty aspiration. They seemed neither plant nor tree, these cacti and joshua trees; nor alive, these clutches of dry grass and sage brush against a rocky ground that gave off a hard glint. The rocks that rose in the distance looked to have no living thing growing on them. Only telephone poles and the blacktop to show that human beings had been here, mainly, Alta thought, to get through it and on to somewhere

12

else: the sort of place you might consider beautiful only if you didn't have to be there.

It was one of those undistinguished spots of blacktop, miles from the notion of a town, they'd come to a halt in the middle of, when the rear axle of the equipment truck broke down, and their little procession came to an uneven halt, like train cars piling up. There was a dull, angry look in the sky, and they'd no sooner got their vehicles pulled off onto the shoulder than the wind picked up the dust and flung it at them, striking the metal roofs and sides like a flail. It was a good thing they weren't going anywhere, because they couldn't have seen to get there anyway. The sun was eclipsed, the windows dark with dust. And though the doors and windows were shut, so they were nearly stifled inside, the dust sifted through anyway, a fine layer over everything. They drank it in their coffee and ate it with their food.

The animals nearly went crazy. The horses neighed and tried to rear in their trailer. The little elephant stamped and trumpeted. The tiger paced her cage all night. And what with the fray and the clatter, the bay gelding had somehow injured a leg. They needed both a vet and a mechanic, two more bills to pay. So it was no wonder that on this day, in what appeared to be the wreckage of the storm, most of the people in the show pulled out. The operators of the booths—little independent outfits that had hooked up with them and would hook on somewhere else. The shooting gallery left, and the lucky spinning wheel, the car races, the coin and ring tossing set-ups—most of the acts and all the games of chance were taking their chances elsewhere.

"Well, you gotta live," Pearl Diamond said when she and Bates, who threw knives at her till her silhouette stood outlined upon the wall and she stepped forth unscathed, were taking off. "Be seeing you," they said to Alta. "No hard feelings." The first to leave, they had put the idea into the common mind, though no doubt somebody else would have thought of it too. Any woman, Alta thought, who trusted a man enough to allow him to throw knives at her was either too dumb or too lucky to have troubles in the world, and she envied her even as she wished her well.

13

If they hadn't missed the turn-off, probably none of this would have happened. They were supposed to have headed north towards Albuquerque, but they'd missed the sign and hadn't had the sense God gave a turnip to stop and look at a map. Before they knew it, they'd gone fifty miles out of their way.

If you hadn't ... And how are we going to get out of this godforsaken place? Money and blame. Bitch, bitch, bitch. As if a man hasn't got enough troubles ... Whose idea was it to ... ? As if you never made a mistake ... Money and blame. I could've made fifty to your one, and we'd both be better off. Brick bats flying back and forth. Pulling your weight ... Whose weight? ... Fed up with your ... Because of you, godammit. You gave me nothing, not even a child ... Couldn't plant anything in that belly of yours except a fart ... I should've got me a better man to try.

The blood had dried on her lip. Tentatively she touched the spot, then turned from the mirror. I could've been ... Not been—was. Was one of the best damn trapeze artists in the business. The two of them together: Gold Dust and Dream Girl. The dream had turned to dust—hah! Ashes to ashes: Gold Dust to Dusty, what a joke. The two of them one great act, till the moment suddenly came, maybe by a slip of the foot and one miss in midair too many, by too dizzying a glance down below, Dusty seemed to lose his nerve, wanted to settle for a life on the ground, but with higher ambitions: a show of his own. At the time when they could've had top billing in "The Greatest Show on Earth," Dusty chased his dream of something grander yet, circus and carnival together, triumphantly called "The Carnival for the Gods." Earth wasn't enough for him.

He was headed into the clouds, into the skyscape of the forever possible, the shape of things to come. They'd play all the big cities, bringing back the days when everybody went to the circus. Giant celebrations in the heart of every city.

But the idea never really got off the ground. It was too vast for anybody but Dusty to believe in for very long. The force of his enthusiasm—he could talk people into anything and they would follow him around with puppylike loyalty—held them for awhile. But starvation was

14

a powerful eye-opener. The shine wore off and off they went. And now they were down to the rag taggle and bob that had stayed because they had nowhere else to go.

There had been better days: when she was up on the high wire, and her body was a flash of motion as she swung, hanging by her heels, across the top of the tent, the faces below like rows of lightbulbs, her body light as a firefly in her blue body suit. All alone up there, no nets below, with the tight thrill that was the joy bred of danger. The tingle in the blood. God, how she loved it! It was the years that had brought her down to earth. She'd nearly killed herself once in a fall. She'd lost her timing, her body had gotten heavy despite all her efforts. The pull of gravity, the reluctance of the flesh. And all the while Dusty trying to put together his misbegotten scheme.

She put some water in the kettle to boil and took out a jar of Sanka. She didn't like the taste much, but even with the heat it was something to put into your mouth and swallow. Something to look into and stir your spoon around in while you sat. She spooned out the instant, poured in the water and sat ruminating, waiting for the coffee to cool, gazing into the dark liquid. Time out. It allowed you to sit down right in the midst of life while somewhere else people were killing each other or having babies or getting the mortgage foreclosed or carrying on a family quarrel that would leave seven people sworn enemies for life. Set a cup of coffee in front of you and none of it mattered, at least for the moment; otherwise you were out scratching and biting and clawing because the world was an obstacle you had to strike out at.

She was full of yearning, but she didn't know what for. When she had had money, she bought clothes, strange fanciful outfits that could have taken her to another age and fashion, or to a costume party. She loved bodices decorated with pearls and sequins and fringes that shimmied when you walked and rhinestones that danced the light. She loved bright colors: reds that could have come from the throat of a trumpet and pinks and oranges and purples that peeled your eyeball back to the optic nerve. She had trousers and a turban made of cloth of gold, and tops all embroidered. Even now, when she took tickets she some-

15

times dressed up as the Queen of Sheba or a priestess of the moon in a gown, her special creation, that shimmered between gold and silver, set off by a crown of rhinestones with a fan of feathers rising from the back. But nobody paid any special attention. She had the stuff all packed in the closet. And Dusty wanted her to get rid of all that rubbish, just taking up space, but it would have been like stripping off her own skin. Yet she knew she'd never wear them anymore. Most of them were too tight anyway.

No, money wasn't good for anything. It was good to spend when you had it, but then you tossed aside what you had bought as so much junk. Dusty still had his ring—so much for the luck it had brought him.

As for love, that was even worse. Had she loved Dusty, she wondered, or had she just wanted a man who dreamed big, was headed for the clouds?

He couldn't even give her a child.

Small wonder he had time to put the makings in her belly, considering where his head always was: scheming and dreaming and adding up columns of figures and charting their course around the country and talking half the night away, too excited even to make love. And though there were ups as well as downs at the beginning, things now were headed in one direction only. It didn't seem to occur to him that they were all washed up. The gaggle of folks they'd picked up was the rout, the survivors who hadn't quite gone over the edge, not the glittering argosy he'd always had in mind. A man with a dream was a madman.

Love. Much worse than money. A giant and a midget who fought and were inseparable. An animal trainer who was convinced a woman lived inside his tiger, the only woman he'd ever wanted. Idly, she wondered if anybody had ever tried fucking a tiger. She'd heard about doing it with cows and sheep and dogs. Probably even with trees, provided you weren't so unlucky as to strike upon a bee hive inside. For all of which, she thought, you'd have to be pretty damn desperate. But a tiger. Even if you could get one to stand still for it, there was something in the nature of a cat that ought to make you a bit leery. You couldn't put your dependence on them. But then the trainer, Sam, was nuts too. Love

16

was too much. It created bizarre obsessions. It was a form of drunkenness and self-abuse. They threatened you with blindness if you twiddled your own organs, or with impotence or insanity. But they should've been smarter than that. Love itself was blind and impotent, insane, and ate the heart away until it was white and leprous and scarred beyond all telling. Never trust it, she thought.

Every once in a while when she needed to feel a little pride in herself, she got dolled up and ran off to have an affair with a truck driver or salesman or drifter who was looking for a little diversion. Men she didn't count on seeing again and usually didn't—or, if she did, the interest had passed. She used to like the thrill in the blood of having a new man, but even that had got old. She didn't trust it anymore, no more than she trusted a greenback. No, neither love nor money had taken her anywhere—just left her here tasting her own blood.

She wanted vaguely to kill somebody, but there wasn't anybody handy and certainly nobody worth the trouble. If it wasn't love and it wasn't money. ... The blood was beating in her veins. It went on beating and beating. Blood, sweat and tears—maybe they were real. She found the water running out of her eyes. Real as dirt. Till you were dirt too. They'd discovered America, and what was it but dirt? She looked outside. The dust had blown off and under the blaze of sun the land was cooking into a piece of burnt toast. Maybe she should go out and start digging, see if she could strike oil. Wouldn't that be a humdinger!

Or maybe she should pull herself together and get up and leave like everybody else. She and Dusty had fought and torn at each other, had driven and goaded and disappointed one another nearly as far as human things can go. And now he'd made her taste her own blood, and she was still here. And what if from now on he made a pleasure of beating on her? Or if she stood for it. ... It made no sense. And if she left ... what would she do? Go wandering through the world, probably, only by herself, waitressing at some cafe or bar. Trying to cadge drinks and lure men home. Even now there'd be snickers behind her back, not to think of the future.

She got up from the table and gave herself to the task of fixing

supper: cut up meat and fried it with sliced onions and put in the to-
matoes and chili peppers and set the pot on the stove to cook. What
with the mechanic and the vet costing an arm and a leg, it might be
the crew's last good meal for a while. Every time you took somebody a
car or a body it seemed they wanted you to set them up for life. She'd
make a big pot of chili that would either tide them over for a couple of
days or feed whoever happened to wander in. Once she'd done that,
she washed her face and cleaned herself up a little. She was needing
company. She'd see what Billy Bigelow was up to.

She could count on him. He'd been with them forever, first as
electrician, carpenter, handyman, what-have-you, and now, after the
defection of Carnaby the Great, he was featured as Bigelow the Magician. He could pull cards from out of people's pockets and from
behind their ears and discover scarves where they hadn't been before.
He had mastered appearance and disappearance and seemed to want
to climb to ever higher steps of illusion. Though sometimes he would
simply take a pile of long thin balloons and blow them up, twist them
into dogs and lions and elephants and kangaroos and send them sailing out into the crowd.

She found him sitting on the couch in his trailer reading
a Time magazine. Probably months or a year old, since Billy never
bought one. But the dates never interested him, it never mattered to
him when an event had occurred.

"Dream Girl," he said, "come on in." He was the only person
who ever called her that, and it seemed to be the only image he'd ever
had of her: up in the air on the high wire. If it were anybody else, she'd
be convinced she was being made fun of.

"Been looking at some moon shots they got here. All crust and
craters."

"My God, why don't you look out the window? Isn't that deso-
late enough for you? If you get up and go outside, you could be on part
of the moon they haven't discovered yet. The lower part."

"You really think the moon looks like this," he asked.

"If it don't, it's missed a bet." She'd come over to joke a bit, but

18

the direction the conversation was taking her, making her think about where she was, only brought on her irritability. She wished Dusty would come back so she could throw something at him.

"You know what I think?" Billy said, taking off his glasses so he could see her more clearly. "I think they go out and take all those pictures and say it's the moon."

"Why'd they do a thing like that? Besides, you got all those rockets going up and men coming down in capsules and stuff."

"Oh, you could fake that." Billy said, with a snap of the fingers. "No trouble at all. Just take a picture, put it alongside another and say it's the moon."

"What on earth for?"

"Because you got to keep one step ahead of the public. You got to keep them wondering, always in suspense. Otherwise they'd get so bored and dull in their minds they'd turn back into tree frogs. There they'd be, rocking back and forth going mumbledyboo and their eyes would go crossed and their lips would droop and pretty soon they'd be squatting in clusters like fungus, just trying to keep the burner going so life wouldn't go out altogether."

"You got some imagination."

"No, I mean it. That's why you got to have carnivals. Probably they got a secret genius agency somewhere with people that do nothing all day and night but think things up, one leap ahead of the rest of us."

"But all you're talking about is plain lies."

"Of course. What other kind is there? Except some lies are plainer than others. People need them, couldn't get along without them. Think about what people have believed, beginning with the earth being flat. All you have to do is get it into their heads and then they swear it's true."

"But now look," she said. "Nobody really believes you find cards behind their ears."

"They'd like to. And if you could convince them you got some leetle secret, they'd believe that too."

He was always playing these games with himself, and she loved the way he twisted everything around till you didn't know whether you were coming or going. She'd lost all her anger. "Well, if everything can be a lie," she said, "then everything can be true just as well." She hadn't the faintest idea what she meant.

"Because people believe it? Then anything can be the truth, can't it? Like all that stuff about living past lives. That could be true."

"Suppose it is. I can't say it isn't. I can't say people haven't been on the moon."

"The people from the future would be living right now, wouldn't they?"

"And how would you know?"

"Use your head. It's got to follow," he said. "And suppose you could go back to the past and you killed your grandfather, would you be alive now?"

"Of course not," she said offhandedly, even though she knew she was being had.

"But then how could you go back ... ?"

"Why weren't you born with two heads?" she wanted to know. "Then one of you could live in the past and the other in the future and tell each other all about it.

"Probably fall flat on my face," he said, "and the present would go leaking through."

"Through the hole in your head." She stopped, all used up. "How come you don't leave like the rest?"

"The show must go on," he said.

"Come on," she said. "What show? This flea-bitten, half-assed ..."

"I love you, Alta—you have such a high opinion of we serious professionals." She couldn't tell if he were teasing her or making fun of himself, or maybe both at once. "I'm a magician."

"And an electrician and a carpenter and—"

"A man of parts," he said.

"Is one of 'em a stomach," she asked. "I've got chili cooking."

"Gotcha."

•

Back in the trailer she stirred the chili, added some oregano and cumin and then sat down to look at the copy of Vogue she'd slipped out of the dentist's office the time she had a toothache in Biloxi.

The sun had really turned on the juice, so she tried to get a little relief by opening the window and turning on the fan. But the flies came in through a tear in the screen and buzzed around her head, and Pansy sat and snapped at them. Now and then she glanced out the window to watch Fred taking care of his horses. He'd taken them out of the trailer one by one and tethered them over by some scrub cedar. He'd brought out hay and water and then had lingered in the heat, grooming them, talking to them, trying to soothe them and make up for a life that offered no explanations, just endless travel, unexpected stops, dust storms, injury and inconvenience—all for the sake of those few triumphant moments in the ring when Ginger, his wife, leapt and danced across their backs.

Every now and then a car or a truck would come whooshing past with a rush of hot air and a slash of light, then go plummeting on into the distance. She had no idea when Dusty would be back. Maybe he'd just taken off like the others. Then a truck—not his—appeared, slowed and finally stopped across the road from the horse trailer. A lean, wiry man got out, took a leather bag from the seat and walked over to where Fred was working with his horses. The vet. As she watched them, a couple of tow trucks pulled up and parked. A burly man, T-shirt sticking to his chest, sunglasses, got out. Then a tall guy, cap on his head, long arms, big hands. Burt, their equipment man, emerged from the rig and came over to talk to them. Then a lot of backing and maneuvering, hauling of chains and attachments. And after a time they were towing the truck away in the direction of what she supposed was a town, though more than likely nothing more than a mirage. She'd believe it when she saw it. But no Dusty.

Then the vet was gone too, and she watched Fred lead the horses back into the trailer. That done, he walked over to the trailer where he

21

lived with Ginger, who leapt from one horse to the other while they raced round the ring, who went up into a handstand or did a flip at the height of their motion, who was beautiful to watch. There was a lightness in her. They deserved better, Alta knew. They were young and, like everybody else who'd been drawn in, had the dream painted in their heads. All full of enthusiasm. Dusty's dream was their dream. She'd seen it happen over and over again. And he wasn't lying when he went on painting the sky in vivid colors. He believed every word of it: it was going to happen. Then, one day, they woke up. He owed them money, like he owed everybody money.

Now she knew they were leaving too. She didn't get up to say goodbye, though she and Ginger had sat in each other's trailers and traded intimacies. And Ginger had showed her bruises on her body in places that didn't show. And sometimes she'd wept: Fred was fonder of his horses than he was of her, treated them better. And to tell the truth, she was sick of the smell of horse. Fred always smelled of horse. Alta didn't go over to say goodbye, because chances were they'd come across each other when they least expected it. In this business you were never surprised.

She felt bad about the money, but there was no help for it. If their paths did cross and Dusty were flush, he'd pay off. That's what he said, and she had no reason to doubt him because so far Dusty hadn't had any money. She watched Ginger climb into the cab of the trailer while Fred went back to drive the one with the horses. Then they were gone. Why wasn't she leaving with them? Was one kind of wandering any worse than another?

For a time she sat there blank and empty, all used up. The anger of the morning seemed as far away as last month. She wasn't even waiting for anything. She turned off the chili, then let the evening move in around her. She sat with her dog in her lap. The deepening sky was a rich blue, a mingling of blues, lighter and dark, with a smoky feeling underneath; it came down into the landscape, softening the edges of the mountains, turning brown slopes to lavender, to indigo, to darker shapes yet that made all of it one vast stillness that reached far beyond her, perhaps to the borders of the world. There were only the little lights of the few trailers left: animal trainer, giant and midget, magician-cum-handyman. That was the carnival now—the scrapings from the pot.

From out of the indigo she saw headlights approach, then heard a truck pull up and stop. She went outside. Dusty was back, but with somebody with him in the front seat. She bent down, leaning on the side of the truck to look in. A girl. She could just about make her out in the gathering dusk. Though she looked to be no more than seventeen-eighteen, she knew everything a woman could know and then some.

"This is Grace," Dusty said, by way of introduction. "Amazing Grace. Wait'll you see what she can do. We'll hit the bigtime yet." I know what she can do, Alta thought. Amazing, all right. Probably one of those street kids that had left home at twelve or thirteen, soon as their periods started and they had their union card for womanhood. Then they peddled it on every street of Everytown in the great U.S. of A. Double A for Amazing. Then she noticed a childish face in the narrow seat behind Dusty. A boy. But so wild he looked like some creature that had been torn away from the land and still carried in its eyes the reflection of the water hole from which it drank, the snug of the nest where it had spent the night still clinging to the fine white hairs on his arms.

"Does he talk," she suddenly asked.

"The words have gone out of him," the girl said, "but the singing has stayed behind. He knows the ballad of Kitty Moreno and Amigo and the Battle of Glorieta Pass and Indian Joe and his fight with a bear and the loves of Pajarito."

These are barely human things, Alta found herself thinking, for she had learned to recognize such and they were not new to her experience. And here was another set in front of her that she might look at and talk to and never understand. She could ask questions till her teeth rotted and it wouldn't make a ghost of a difference. There they were, almost cringing in the seat of the truck. In the back with the boy, she noticed two crates that looked to be the dimensions of their personal property and inside which something stirred and moved with a vaguely animal and somewhat sinister quality. She didn't ask what.

23

"You want something to eat," she asked, for she could recognize hunger too, though on what level she couldn't always tell. "I've got a pot of chili on the stove."

They stepped out of the truck, the girl rubbing her arms against the evening chill. Alta saw a square of light as the door of Billy Bigelow's trailer opened. He'd be coming too.

She looked off into the distance before she went inside: over in the mountains it looked as though a storm was brewing up. A sudden flash of lightning and the mountains stood out, every slope and draw outlined in angular crossings of brilliance. If it rains, she thought, it will pick up the dust and the sky will fall down in mud. First they'd nearly been swept away, now it was more than likely they'd be mired down. Or else the water could come tearing down the mountains in a flash flood.

"Come on inside," she said, and went to the stove to put the fire on. Dusty was still fiddling outside in the truck while these two stood uncertainly in the doorway. "You can wash up in there," she said. The boy's eyes went roaming around the trailer as if it would take getting used to. Alta went about setting the table.

Here they were, just another pair among the number she had seen in the procession of all the broken, ill-formed, misbegotten things headed out of the world and onto the road, moving from town to town, never calling any place their own. They were her family, if you could call it that—they were her fate.

She closed the front door. It was getting cold now as night took over the desert. She was closing the door against the night, against the rustle of lizards and the spines of cactus, against whatever shapes lay in the darkness and whatever moved in the silence. Then Billy Bigelow and Dusty came in talking about the day. Only the sound of voices and the smell of chili seemed warm and real.

24

Small Wonder

The letter arrived innocently enough, without so much as a return address. A fan letter— Curran hit on it at first glance. Seldom did they come, but when one appeared, his ears tingled, a pleasant flutter rippled across his midriff, his mind did a little dance. Recognition. Ah, hit me again, lads. Et maintenant, Mesdames et messieurs, je vous presente: le Grand Curran. (Naturally it would be in French.) And now once more: from the woman who'd watched his act three nights in a row, so hot for the performance not even a kid in tow gave her an excuse to revel in the high jinx. He was sure of it: the woman who'd staged her own disappearing act as soon as his and Donovan's was over. He didn't know why she'd struck him that first night as he scanned the audience. No prize certainly. Blowsy: a blown poppy. Bleached hair, painted lips, a certain hectic quality in the cheeks. A face ravaged yet familiar, like a tune, a taste that teases one out of mind. And when she returned the next night, he was not only flattered, but eased, confirmed. His performance mattered. He directed it toward her like a kiss blown in her direction, to the mystery woman who'd come just for him. A gift: he was at the top of his form, making them clap till their hands ached. Even Donovan said as much—quite an admission from the old jaguar. In the old days you'd have had to goose him with a red-hot poker to win even a grunt of approval.

In this season of largesse, in the glow of late summer, Curran indulged himself in a few well-earned fantasies—why let Donovan hog them all? So he was humanity writ small: that much more to prize. Royalty had graced its courts with midgets and dwarfs, recognizing a quality so special it was given place among the anointed. Hadn't the great Velasquez painted them? Goya as well. Immortal now. What the populace had cast aside had been rescued, given blessing. Freaks no longer. As for himself, he hugged a long-cherished ambition. Not to have his portrait painted—but to create one of his own, at least as large as life.

He put the envelope to his nose in the hope of scent, breathed in an indifferent paper smell, and unfolded a piece of lined notebook paper. As soon as he read the first words, the blood thrummed in his temples. No wonder, no wonder. He didn't have to look to the signature. So she'd come back once more to haunt him.

Dear Edward, he read. So she'd always addressed him. Formal. Serious. Not Eddie or Weebit or Shortstuff. Nothing a twenty-year-old who had the goods, so to speak, might lay on him the way everybody else did. Oh no, there were better ways to make a satire of him. Edward. Call it her unique brand of affection. As with his parents, a sort of euphemism for the scrap of humanity fate had presented them with. Who would never grow beyond his four feet one inch. Generous of nature that extra inch. Largesse.

There's a tooth missing in front, so I'm not keen on giving out with those million-dollar smiles. One more thing missing in this witch's brew we call life. Do you know folly, do you know madness? I got my arms plunged in to the elbows. Think of when you knew me. What I had when I was young! Taking my good-natured stretch in all that bilking innocence. Then you get socked a few wallopers. Changes your mind about a few things.

Yes, think of her back then. A poppy flaring open. How he'd loved her—ascending joyfully in the fruit-fly moment. And for what? So that she could throw herself away. Elise: as sylph-like as her name. Her image still lived with him: the cameo face framed by the chestnut hair, a face he wanted only to frame in memory. But let go of that; only think of her body in motion. For bones, she had light waves. One more touch and she'd have been a creature of air. The equal of any Chinese acrobat—the highest praise he could confer on her. She should have been a feature act in the circuses both of the U.S. and Europe—he was convinced of it. And she had thrown it all away. For love! Women had a way of doing that—but not in his direction.

26

Now even her name didn't fit.

So now you have me—a missing tooth and a smoker's hack. You've seen me— Gay S. Who— I saw that eye of yours dart out and scoop me in. Saw your name on the boards when we hit town. Had to see you. What am I here for—shall she tell? I couldn't make it to the dressing room, though I kept trying. The rotgut gets you primed, then it gives you a kick in the slats. It's this son of mine. You saw him that day I came. A cute little kid.

A shudder ran through him.

Only now madder than any of us, madder than a clown. My hands are empty, clawing air. What am I asking? Come, if you got nothing better to do. You liked me well enough once, though I'm not fixing any claims on you. And you've got the past against me.

That was bad enough, let alone the rest. He couldn't even think about the boy, the revenge he'd taken on him just for being there that day they came to visit. It was she who'd opened a vein: what she'd done to herself, when he was ready to dedicate his every corpuscle to her talent. Not like Dusty, who wanted to soar to the heights on everybody else's wings. The Big Man. But he'd have done anything for her, just to get her go on thrilling audiences the way she thrilled him. Only let him forget it—if he didn't stop himself he'd be playing the score of old resentments.

Remember Orlando. That loudmouth. I could kill that mother. If he knew what I was up to he'd have my hide. And Tamilla—she runs things now. No sweetheart, let me tell you. But I don't care. I know all their tricks and connivings. They have a use for madness all right. They'll take it for a gift.

Orlando. The Juggler. Throwing pins into the air beyond the catch of the eye, until he made a mad circle of them, whirling flashes of shape, with a can't-catch-me—only he himself throwing and catching. Followed by plates and hoops, whatever might sail into the air for that brief second of equipoise. And when you were left breathless, he tossed himself forward with a laugh and an armful of hoops. Once in place, he set them alight, spurting beer into the flames until they roared upward; then he went leaping through. Big Orlando. Muscles running all over his arms—very likely up to his head. Muscles for brains. And so pleased with himself, he could have kissed his own ass. The way he'd glance down and say, Hey squirt, why don't you climb out of that hole? Stroking his beautiful mustache as he strode away. Turning only once when Curran threw him a finger and fantasized about butting him in the groin. Nothing could touch him.

Inevitably, they married. Yet Orlando was jealous enough to pull his prize away from the outfit at the end of the season, as if Curran's presence could make the least possible difference. He didn't even want them talking to each other. Made her leave behind all her friends, juggling her in only one direction—his own. He'd already had one wife to bully—used her up and cast her off. So rumor had it. And here came another hapless young thing to fall for him. Not even Alta had been able to warn her off. Maybe it was a good thing they left; Curran could exchange the torment of seeing her for the torment of her absence. Her career ended there: she had a kid, a girl. Sick a lot, she wrote him. She lost her sometime during the first year. Took the heart out of her. Then the boy came. Until she'd turned up with the kid to visit him that afternoon Curran was ashamed to think of now, he'd had scarcely a word of what had happened to her during those intervening years. Hadn't wanted to know. She'd quit writing, just sent him a post card now and then. Thinking of you. Thinking. Little objects and pictures kept arriving. Oddities. Relics. An ashtray made of a shark's eye socket. A little set of enameled boxes that fit one inside the other. In the last, she'd placed the tiniest seashell. Donovan couldn't resist the chance to rib him about her. She's got the hots for you, kid. That would put him in a lather for a week. He'd never answered those missives. Never a return address. He'd try to make out the name of the town from the postmark; usually it was a blur. Texas, he made out once. Arkansas. Then she

28

dropped from sight. What?—five or six years ago. No, after the visit.

Tamilla he didn't know about—the name didn't ring any bell. Nor did he speculate much about that part of the past, the second part, with its odd kinks and detours, its stretches of obscurity that now turned into the present. Only what he'd shared with her, with its small gleams and lights—a word, a touch here and there—juxtaposed with a present entirely at odds with it.

Confronted with the debris, the images he'd have gladly cast off, he found them as unreal as anything under the spotlights. Like everything around them. Like the resort hotel they had the run of this round, thanks to the bankruptcy proceedings it was mired in. They were living high, frolicking in a decor like cotton candy that required only the reek of elephant, lion, horse, or the day's headlines to give you a measure of its insubstantiality. In the pink—that's what it meant. In the lap of Lady Bountiful. Here he was—one who'd created illusions all his life, soaking up the sense of his value as he played in their midst. He looked outside to where a few golfers were teeing off on the green, retirees, sporty in their caps and corduroys, who'd take their boats out on the Gulf later in the day. The carnival had landed here too—for the season's last gig, to spin one more set of illusions before the costumes were packed away.

Well, come along for the ride if you have the stomach for it.

The letter ended there on the raw edge of her words. The name of the town in northern Mexico they quartered in—very likely as poverty-infested as it was picturesque—was scribbled across the bottom. Otherwise leaving him in the dark of his own thoughts. A son gone out of his head . . . How had it happened and what did she imagine her Edward could do about it? Double over in the throes of the past? Come and scout the act? Why had she singled him out? To get some oblique sort of revenge? He could almost believe it. Hardened and quirky though she was, she wouldn't have been a real woman if she couldn't get her hooks into his hide. When push came to shove, they could always zero in on the mechanics or the mathematics of getting what they wanted out of you, her misery the only invitation to his company. Get that. And the logic behind it—

29

Because now he couldn't simply tear up the letter, throw it away and pretend it had never come—an event unborn. Fan letter. He held it in front of him like a scorpion. Why not just toss it down? Now you see it, now you don't. The old magic of survival, and the easiest escape route in the world. But she would haunt him. Love, the old monster departing, always left behind its smelly hide. Her voice was already buzzing in his ear, the hard-edged cant of it. Even so, he would read the words over a dozen times, though they would not tell him one whit more.

He was desperate for a cup of coffee. Where should he put the damned thing, get it out of his sight. Unless he hid the letter carefully, Donovan was sure to come upon it, in that uncanny way he had of sniffing things out, particularly the ones that laid you open—pretending it wasn't worth his while, but all the same priming himself to rib you later on. Curran went to the bureau and shoved the letter inside one of his socks. But it seemed to announce itself immediately: Psst. Over here, bub. Any hiding place he fixed on burned itself into his mind as the first place Donovan would notice. He folded the letter, slipped it into his shirt pocket and left the room.

In the hall, the maid stood with her cart, taking up sheets and towels for the room next to his. "Mornin', Mr. Munchkin," she said "You with that circus outfit landed here?"

He was ready to snarl at her, but her face held such innocent good will, he stopped short.

"I never did see a real live circus person," she said.

"What makes you think you're seeing one now?"

She studied him. "You mean you just an ordinary midget."
He had to laugh. He liked the eager rhythm in her body, the large curious eyes. He was ready to tilt words and glances with her. A little act. "You've caught me. The secret's out. You're looking at the world's greatest little performer."

"That right? That's what I'm looking at?" She knew what he was about. Her brow creased. A considering pout came to her lips. "Think it might be worth my while putting out for a ticket?"

"It's the Carnival for the Gods, honey." He elaborated with his

30

hands. "You can't think any bigger than that." It took a leap beyond the ordinary; he could only make the suggestion.

She gave a little flick of the wrist.

"I done heard all that stuff before."

"Yeah," he acknowledged with a shrug. "It's hard to believe. They've run out of words for the real thing—just run them into the ground. Can't see for the looking. "Well," he concluded, "you'll have to take your chances. And you've got only one. Tonight's the last perfor- mance. One thin line between seeing it and missing it—maybe forever."

"Like getting married."

"Or taking a job in Australia."

Both stood considering the sleight of hand that played with even ordinary possibilities. "Some of them outfits you'd be doing yourself a favor to miss," she said. "And then every once in a while . . . Like some special you get on t.v. All the beautiful costumes. All those acrobatics you can't imagine anybody doing except the Chinese." She riveted him with her gaze. "You like doing that circus stuff?"

"It's a living," he granted.

"I'd give everything for that kind of life," she said. "Or else win- ning the lottery. I'd have me a ball." Her eyes went wild. "You wouldn't have to lift a finger. Just go dancing." She did a little shimmy, snapping her fingers. "Now that's what I'd call being lucky." She turned back to his situation. "All the folks out there just to watch what you do. Clap- ping." She shook her head. "Want to watch me make a bed?" She laughed. "They clapped for me once when I got a good citizen award. Think of that." She paused. "Gave one to everybody that didn't pack a knife."

"Something to clap for all right."

She wasn't going to settle for his irony. "Come on now."

He had to admit it—nothing sweeter to his ears, the swell of sound from an appreciative crowd. His reward for being what he was. What he did was better than most things he could think of doing. Bet- ter than changing sheets. Though there were moments enough when he wondered what anybody could envy him for—If she could have been in the right place at the right time, a figure kneeling, eyes half-lidded and breasts pointed out, she'd have been praised for suggesting the delights of the earth. Now she was pushing her cart in the direction of his room. Yet if he assailed her with a flourish, "Hey Sweetheart, let's you and me do the town tonight," she wouldn't laugh in his face—he was too short for that—she'd pour laughter on his head. "Honey, I'd have to pick you up like a kid and dance you around. I got to find somebody to do me some good." Worse if she took him up for the novelty of it. No, leave it alone. Let them stand inside their separate doorways looking out.

He gave her a wave and took off down the hall. Right now he loved the life. Other days it was a flop you wanted to spit on, the pile-up of all your mistakes and failures. But then you could figure on that, sure as the holes in your socks. At the end of the best season he'd had in years, here came the letter to snatch the heart right out of him. As though he owed her anything . . .

Halfway to the coffee shop he came to a halt. In all the furor over the letter, which he'd picked up at the desk not ten minutes before, he'd forgotten what he'd really intended to do that morning—indulge his secret passion, work on his memoir while Donovan was off putting the final touches to the arrangements for the party after their last performance.

"Forgot something," he said, hustling past the maid.

"I'm definitely going," she said.

"The thrill of a lifetime." He was fumbling with the key.

"You autograph my program?" she said.

He looked up. "Me and my partner too," he said magnanimously. "The tall one."

"Hey, if you're ever on t.v., I can say I knew you. Can I touch you?"

"You might catch something you couldn't get rid of."

She looked at him dubiously. "What you carrying around?"

Longing, he could have said. The worst of all afflictions.

Inside the room, he brought out his notebook from the back pocket of his suitcase. Over the years, as the cover grew more battered and the spine loosened, the bulge in the middle had expanded. A little like himself. Now the thing was a weight to carry around. He hardly knew what he had stuffed into it. The one thing he didn't have was a title, and he was stuck for an opening. The pressure was rising. He needed a slant, a hook to hang it on—his life. Something catchy for the public he aspired to reach. A restless and amorphous public, to be converted somehow into a receptive and eager one. As he went downstairs again, he at least had in his hands the instrument to distract him from Elise and her troubles. Damn her for the interruption just when, he was convinced, he was on the verge of a real breakthrough.

He turned into the coffee shop. Deserted—nothing to distract him. Alta and Dusty were working on the balance sheet; some of the troupe were off rehearsing, and those who had nothing pressing to do had gone down to the beach to walk in the white sand or take a dip. He hadn't yet made up his mind about the letter, but in his heart of hearts he wanted someone to convince him not to go. He and Donovan were supposed to travel together to Jamaica. After such a season, they owed it to themselves. Nobody could blame him—they already had their tickets. Maybe he'd say a word to Alta later on—she'd put his mind at ease. He took a table by the window so that he could look out over the bayou alongside the hotel and ordered coffee. One of the waiters had tried to joke him into believing it was crawling with alligators big enough to devour him with a single snap of the jaws. Big laugh. Still he didn't walk too close.

He lingered over his coffee, glancing toward the book now and then as though a current of inspiration might suddenly surge out of it. Finally he pushed the cup aside, took out a pen, and readied himself for struggle. All his life, it seemed, he'd been trying to write a book. At first, it was a meager affair, a sketchy and random list of facts just for the record—the where and when of places they'd been, what he'd done. These he recorded in pencil, as though his sense of their significance had been in doubt. The entries had faded with time and were now hard to make out. As he went along certain events kept bobbing above the ordinary. Taking the odd turn. Cavorting into the freakish. These

33

he recorded zealously, trying indeed to develop a whole system of the peculiar, no doubt to give himself company. But at some point, the focus shifted. He started giving more attention to his surroundings, to the interplay between himself and other performers and the audience. His reactions, descriptions. The world of Carnival. He'd found himself grabbing up scraps of paper, even napkins, and jotting things down. These now lay in loose chaos between the covers. What to do with it all.

A Memoir—that was his dream now. True, everybody was writing memoirs. Panting to spill the goods: not just rock stars and movie idols and former CIA agents and those who'd won mega bucks in real estate. But firemen careering to the rescue; tattoo artists inscribing ships and serpents and flying horses and butterflies on the arms and torsos of Danish sailors and feminists; chefs who'd concocted fabulous dishes, particularly out of tofu; dancers and astrophysicists and preachers. Soapbox orators; Aerobics teachers. The used and the abused. The lucky and unlucky in love. Winners of lotteries. Con men. Terrorists and sex maniacs. Those who'd been cheating the public in the style of S&L robber barons. Do something illegal enough or depraved enough, beyond scandal enough, and publishers and TV producers and Hollywood moguls came running at you waving checks in the six figures. Reporters flocked about with their cameras and recorders. College presidents courted you for lecture circuit. From prison you could be a celebrity. All for those with stories to tell. Why not himself? He had to bank on being insignificant enough to make a difference.

He opened an ordinary scrapbook and began leafing through collages of programs, some from the Carnival, a number from circuses in which he'd been a guest performer. Scraps now, but still they held a certain power. Like mirrors in which to find himself. He'd even had a couple of offer's he'd turned down. Imagine! He'd stuck it out with the Carnival, watched it rise and fall and rise again, literally from the flames, his career tied to its fortunes. He and Donovan were still together, though it was a miracle they'd avoided strangling one another. And before he was done he'd have to say something about all of them, Donovan in particular, who'd played the big to his small. Now he racked his brain for a title. Something catchy. Try This On For Size. Maybe a little abstract, if not a trifle vulgar. He tapped his pen on the table top.

His claim to fame had to do with smallness. The shape of that smallness. The genius of it, to be sent in the direction of laughter, the unforgettable—shaped for the hearts of thousands. Wonderful, full of wonder. Wasn't that what Carnival was about? And then it came to him. The focus, the title. Small Wonder.

He was so pleased with himself he immediately signaled the waitress. Let her implement his mood of celebration: a cup of hot chocolate this time, and the pastry with the apricot filling he'd admired in the case. Ordinarily he didn't indulge himself, he had to watch the calories; but here was a special occasion. He saw before him a way to go, past the scraps and clippings, the chaos of observations. He knew what he wanted, a special significance to these events. A true sense of what life had been in this body, with this mind, presented with certain opportunities and not others. But to be done with a flourish as well. After all, light and color and gesture went into a portrait as much as a performance. The upsweep of invention. He aspired to realize a world in its vividness, real enough that you felt saturated by its colors. The fabulous—carnival and circus were full of it. In some sense he was quite as fabulous as anything invented, including the unicorn.

He scratched around with his pen for a moment. "I was born .. " Everybody could make the same claim. The sine qua non. He had to do better. He couldn't rely on the rise from rags to riches, nor, as yet, from obscurity to fame. And the I had begun to bother him. He didn't want the portrait to be shoved aside by the painter. He wanted to be able to step back and see what his brush had accomplished.

He started again. To his eager parents the birth of a son was like the appearance of Tom Thumb. Nice idea, but it had already been done. Colonel Tom Thumb, so gilded with fame by P.T. Barnum. Gracing the courts of royalty indeed, the marriage to his midget bride mobbed by well-wishers. Curran had to confess his own adventures lacked something of that pizzazz, nor could he go back to those of the clever inchling who had foiled thieves and emerged from cow's stomach and wolf's maw. His own parents had finally had to take him out of school so the kids wouldn't pick on him. And there were those anxious visits to doctors for the miracle drug that would inspire him to grow. His adventures. The time he was assailed by the young toughs in Ventura City and had escaped by hiding in a barrel. The time he was nearly trampled by an elephant. The fire in Old Town. Images crowded his mind. And the ringing laughter they'd both sought for.

Like Tom Thumb he had his struggles. He wrote eagerly for the next hour, but when he read over what he'd written, he seemed to have missed the point. Obstacles in his path. Obstacles to what? Did that put him alone on the planet? He could scarcely remember back to when he'd gone sailing out into each new morning, eager, ready to climb the trees up into it. He'd had to watch while all around him the children had grown up into their lies, leaving him to the unreality of himself. What was the child father to? A man, yet not a man. A manikin, a Munchkin. Except for that one brief moment at the festival in the Seven Cities when he'd been taken back into some part of experience he hardly knew existed, or whether it belonged to childhood or manhood. Both he'd had to put aside for him to fashion himself into something called a midget. Where the worst of child and man had met—to give him entrance into the world he occupied. Being good for a laugh. Making a joke of being.

But all that you forgot in the effort to get the performance out there, no matter how bad things were, the toothache or the love ache splitting your head. Only the antic play for the crowd you hoped would be jamming the bleachers, you riding their reactions like waves. Forget the accidents and missteps that got in the way: money troubles, animals going lame, quarrels breaking out, prima donnas giving everybody the fits. No end to them. And yet always beckoning beyond the tawdriness of circumstance—the dream. The dream that somehow it all made a difference. Maybe the most fantastic dream of all. CARNIVAL FOR THE GODS—what he claimed to be part of. He gazed out the window for some moments. What he'd bitten off was more than he'd bargained for. All the stuff lying in the pot, the ingredients of what sort of dish?

36

As he stared out the window, absorbed, his attention was caught almost before he was aware of it, by a shape, a set of curves. A heron standing at the edge of the little ragged bayou just under the window. He'd never seen one so close, and he let go of what was in his mind to trace the curve of the head, the shape of the body, the stilt-like legs—all in the service of its fixed and attentive pose. Waiting. Everything invested in waiting. Then a quick movement. Dipping into the water, the heron came up with a sizeable fish, wriggling silver in the sun. Held it in its beak and began swallowing it. A brief distension of the gorge and the fish was gone. The heron dipped again for a swallow of water to wash down the meal. Then it waded to another spot, picking up the hinged sticks of its legs—perfect for the water, a handicap on land—and again stood still, attentive, occasionally wading to another spot. As Curran observed, he seemed to enter into its watching, to watch with it. So caught up was he in the heron's concentration, he could have been the heron fishing, his whole being focused. His attention burned the surface of the water, alive to any pulsation in it. He stepped with those stilts of legs. Then suddenly the bird flew off and with a little jolt he was on the other side of the moment.

He closed his notebook. Heron. Heron fishing. Lucky creature: all it had to do was be itself. Unfortunate for the fish that made it possible.

Dancing with Snakes

Part I.

Lights all a-dazzle. Dancing across the marquee like a comet's tail. That's me. Amazing. Featured act here at the new Las Vegas nightspot—Galactic Explosions, the latest shows a play of colored lights and images that whirl your mind to worlds beyond imagination. I get to show my stuff here and in Atlantic City and Miami too, plus an offbeat little place in L.A. The rest of the time I travel with the circus, where I'd rather be. The glitz pays the bills and allows me to save up for my education. My great dream is to go to college and discover other worlds there. I've got lots to learn; I have to make up for lost time.

So tonight I'll step out onstage in my favorite costume, red and gold, sequins and rhinestones on the outside, me on the inside. Then with well-timed consideration, I remove my veils and girdles and get down to the real thing—me in my bikini, giving a shimmy, getting the parts moving before inviting the snakes to appear. There's a gasp from the audience—count on it. That's my cue. And I'm on, doing my dance.

What a way to earn a living, you say. But I'm off into the excitement that holds me breathless, moving with the snakes as they move with me, and maybe you'll get caught up in the wave, into the thrill and fear that clutches at the midriff—that takes you to the edge.

Amazing all right. But that's not the half of it. Even more amazing is how I got here in the first place, counting all that happened along the way. And I'm not here for keeps. I'm biding my time. There's a special person I'm waiting for, to come and tell me his story. Meanwhile, hang on, and you'll know all.

Snakes? Some people are scared spitless by the very mention of them, let alone having one crawl over your skin. Once I read about the Hopi Indians, how they gather snakes and let them crawl all over their bodies as they sit in the kiva, calm and steady as a cedar post. Then they dance with them—rattlers and sidewinders, with their fangs and poison. They call them "Brother." And after the celebration, they let them go.

Though I, too, felt a stab of fear at first, I came to feel a kinship. Like they lived inside me. Whatever drew me towards the snakes lived in my childhood before I was able to reach for words to tell about it.

When I was a kid, I hardly had a name. It felt like I was kin to animals. Maybe that was on account of something you couldn't give a name to—a wildness that lived in us both without my seeing any difference. I just preferred to get down under the table with the dog or the cat, or go chasing after a rabbit in the weeds.

There wasn't a whole lot then to tie me to the human. I couldn't remember anyone calling me by a syllable that drew me to the sound, made me want to take it on. Oh, I might hear, "Hey you," or "Get on over here, you little stinkweed." This from the one who stood in for a father, if he stood anywhere at all. Not that I ever called him Daddy. A mouth, that's what he was, all scrunched up like he'd bit off too much of life and wanted to spit out the taste before he choked on it.

His name was Priam Gillespie. He hated that name, the way people pronounced it Pry-am or Pree-am. Every once in a while somebody would say, "What the hell kind of name is that?"

"It's what comes of having a librarian for a mother," he'd explain. "Damn her hide anyway."

Every once in a while, maybe in a store or the bank, somebody would call him Mr. Gillespie, and I'd look around for the stranger I thought they were speaking to. Sometimes he called me Miss or Missy. "Don't give me any of that guff, Missy." Or "Toots" when I was coming on to being a woman. "Oh, so now you're getting ready to strut your stuff, eh Toots." I wanted to kick him.

Somewhere there was a birth certificate with my paper name but it just fell by the way—it had nothing to do with me. Whenever somebody spoke it, I didn't look around or say a word. "What's your name, honey?" some folks would ask, and when they drew a blank, they'd smile down into my face, as if getting closer would turn on the light bulb, and ask,

"What's your dolly's name?" It wasn't a real doll, just a sock with stuffing in it, and button eyes and a mouth sewed on. "Name," I'd tell them. "Name—that's her name?" That would tickle them all right.

And Priam would say, "She's just ornery—always has been." Maybe Ornery could have been my name.

"Just wait till I can send you over to Texas," he'd say every once in a while, like he was trying to get even with me—"and let that mama of yours do what she was created for." And then under his breath, "If she'd quit running around long enough to do anything useful."

A voice from long ago ran like a tune through my head: I could remember someone holding my hand. I could almost feel the way it curled around mine—warm and a little moist—even when I couldn't attach a person to it. Was that my mama? I couldn't see her—I was never sure. I really couldn't remember any mama at all. Seems like I'd just happened in this place, like a scrap of paper blown in by the wind.

Every once in a while I'd ask when I was going to Texas, but Priam would pull a face and say, "Mind your business. I got troubles enough as it is."

It took me a while to get a name, as I'll tell you, and it happened in a way I never expected. That seems the way of things—full of surprises. My life started changing when I was about eleven—when Priam got hold of a piece of land across the highway. Took it for collateral from a Mexican family who'd got into his clutches.

I used to play horse with their kids, and Carolina and I liked to braid each other's hair. Hers was long and black and glossy, and I loved to get my fingers in it. Sometimes I'd eat dinner in their adobe hut—tortillas with beans, and enchiladas with red chili sauce, and sopapillas with honey. I can almost taste the food yet—the chili hot in my mouth, then the sweet taste of the sopapillas—and the way Carolina's mama filled my plate and teased me and treated me like one of her own kids. The day they all left, I stood there like a stone, watching them pack up their truck with boxes and baskets, lifting up the couch, then the kids piling in, lining up on it, their dog in the middle, a friendly brown mutt with a long body and little short legs named Chico, who was always part of our games. Then

41

they were gone in a cloud of dust.

"Vaya con migo. Vaya, amiga. Muy lejos de aqui." Let me grab my stick and trot my pony—ta da, ta da, ta da.

Their adobe hut sat empty for I don't know how long, the wind shuffling a few tumbleweeds and scraps of paper in its direction. A little way off were some dilapidated sheds and corrals that had once kept horses or cattle, plus an abandoned shack that people said was haunted by the ghost of Geronimo. I never figured out what he'd be doing there in the neighborhood unless he was really down on his luck. But us kids had played like he was still inside and whoever saw him gave out a yell and took off. I never saw him, but I pretended I did and yelled and ran with the rest.

Just opposite was our place with its peeling adobe and rusting truck parts and junk scattered around the yard. Priam outside lying in the hammock or sitting in a rocker that no longer rocked, wearing down the day crabbing about the heat or cussing the dog or kicking the cat, whatever had the misfortune to cross his path, while a few dusty chickens pecked at what they could come by among the weeds.

One day after a cloudburst had turned the yard to mud, a beat-up black truck pulled into the ruts at the edge of the place, and a fellow unfolded himself from inside and made his way around the mud over to where Priam was sitting under the box elder, the only shade—a scrawny fellow with a high forehead, cleft chin, and a snaggle tooth when he grinned. He stuck out a bony hand to offer a handshake and said, "Howdy, I'm Tiger Higgins and I hear you own that piece of property there across the blacktop."

Priam looked him up and down. "What's it to you?"

"I got a business proposition—that's what."

"Prime land. Make you a fortune in the cattle business," Priam fired back. "I been waiting for the right investment."

"Looks to me like a grasshopper would starve over there. But I'll make you an offer you can't refuse. "

I could tell Priam didn't believe a word of it, but the smell of a deal set the juices flowing. After a session of jawing and jockeying, sweating and swearing, the two of them landed in roughly the same spot, and afterwards Priam even offered the fellow a shot of whiskey. Money changing from somebody's palm into his own always pumped him up for at least three days.

A couple of weeks of feverish activity—tearing out rotted posts and boards, hammering and nailing, repairing sheds and fence posts, putting up metal bars and attaching chain link fence and the place looked pretty good. Then a sign went up. Roadside Zoo—Animals from the Wild. Exotic. Thrilling. The Jungle brought to your very doorstep.

The jungle—in the midst of that stretch of yucca and cactus and mesquite. The idea seized hold of my imagination—the biggest thing to happen since third grade. Once I'd learned to read and do arithmetic, Priam figured I had all the learning I would ever need to make my way in the world. The rest you could get from TV—though ours offered up mostly snow and static. Meanwhile he'd find enough to keep me busy.

I wanted to hang around and watch the goings-on—and a couple of times Tiger let me hand him nails and tools—fun stuff—while he told me about tracking animals and how you had to show the big cats who was boss But after a couple of days Priam came and fetched me home.

"He ain't open yet, Missy—you can do a look-see later on." So I watched from the other side, when I wasn't taking care of the chickens or sneaking off to the arroyo to look for rocks with fossils in them. I found a neat book once in the school library showing creatures that had once lived when the world was new and the mountains were the bottom of the sea.

One day I got to go over and pick up the beer cans and whiskey bottles and paper cups and pieces of plastic that had been tossed out from passing cars and landed in each other's company. Tiger paid me a dollar and a half and gave me a soda. The place was beginning to look halfway decent.

The next day a big trailer-truck pulled up. Tiger and a couple of helpers, a high school kid—big square fellow, Greg—and the other, Ralph, older but strong, who acted like he knew about animals, opened up the back and started unloading cages and crates and leading out the animals. They hefted a cage with a tiger onto a trolley, then another, with a young one, hardly more than a kit. I'd never seen a real live tiger before, never

43

seen wild animals up close. And here came a leopard, an ocelot, a cougar. I got goose bumps all down my arms.

Then came the dog types—coyote, fox and dingo. Some of the animals were new to me—I had to learn what they were. They led a camel into the yard, who passed it over with a sneer. I could see monkeys, even a zebra. There were birds too. A couple of gaudy parrots, a big white cockatoo. Finally some wooden crates labeled "reptiles."

Lights had been strung up along with the signs. GRAND OPENING. Special family rate—little kids free. For a while things were hopping. People pulling in to look at the zoo and stop at the stand to buy a soda, some chips or popcorn, or get a bag of food for the animals. "You get folks involved," Tiger said, "—keeps down the overhead that way." He tapped his head to show how full it was of smarts. When the place closed up for the day, Tiger came over with a bottle of whiskey, and he and Priam poured it out into two orange juice glasses and lifted them to the future.

Tiger had a gold mine, nothing less, and he was full of plans now that he was on his feet again. Bad luck a while back with some of his animals over in Oklahoma. But he'd bought up a new supply from a couple of zoos selling off their surplus and their elders. Now he was going to breed tigers again—He was waiting for the young female to get to where he could breed her. Once he'd bred over twenty tigers—that's how he'd got his name—and sold them all to folks that practically stood in line for one of the kits. A huge market for all he could produce. "You can't imagine—all the folks wanting their own tigers—and ocelots and leopards, but especially tigers." He was one big cockeyed grin, and the two of them kept at that bottle till they were chummy as blood brothers.

After I'd nagged him till he was ready to tear his hair or mine, Priam took me over to see the animals. The cages were all lined up, the cats all together, the monkeys in their own spot, and the coyote, fox and dingo—dog types—in theirs. It was the little tiger that won my heart. I stood in front of her until I could feel Priam's impatience coming at me in a hot blast.

I hated to leave her. She just sat there looking around, bewildered, uncertain, like she'd found herself in a strange place and didn't know what to do. I could tell from her eyes.

44

The other cats acted like they knew exactly where they were and kept pacing from one end of their cages to the other. No wonder. Hardly enough room for them to turn around. The lion was in a different space—didn't budge all the time we were there, just lay in the sun with eyes half-lidded.

More action with the monkeys. They were moving all the time. Each had a swing, but they couldn't swing very far, so they took to hanging and swinging all along the sides. The parrots sat on their perches picking at their feathers. Every once in a while the cockatoo let out an ear-splitting shriek.

"Let's go home," I said. My head was full of noise and smells, and I had a sinking feeling I couldn't give a name to.

"Now hold on," Priam said. "You had ants in your pants to get over here. And I got to see to my investment. I want a look at what's inside."

Inside were the reptiles, and a slimy smell. A big turtle sat on a little pile of dirt in a circle of stones, a pan of water nearby. To keep it company a pair of rattlers were draped over a dead branch not far away. Then in the next tank I saw a circle of thick coils spiraled around until they pointed forward into a dark head with a white stripe in the middle. The coils had wiggly black and yellow strips that made a pattern. Beautiful to look at, but it made me dizzy and sent chills down my spine. I held my breath.

"That's a python," Ralph said as he was setting things up. He'd just finished putting a heating pad under the tank. "Carpet python. How'd you like that for a pet?"

I could feel something coming from inside it that nobody could claim. Different from the cats. I felt I knew them as soon as I laid eyes on them. All their fierceness. Proud. Dangerous. But I had the feeling they knew how to dream. I wanted to get to know the cats. I wasn't sure about the snakes.

The python just fixed me to the spot, not giving anything away. Looked like it was curled around something calm but cold, like nothing would dare to bother it. Made me feel how jittery I was.

"If they trust you, they're easy to handle," Ralph said, maybe to reassure me. "Only you have to be careful. If they're hungry, they'll strike at anything that moves and throw their coils. The big ones can kill a man."

He would have gone on talking about them, but Priam hauled me off so that Tiger could show us the rest of his critters, as he called them. We threaded through the kids with their popcorn and sodas and bags of animal food, and their moms and dads. But I'd seen all I wanted, and kept pulling at Priam's arm till he was ready to slap me. "Go on home then," Priam said. "You make me tired."

"Wait a minute," Tiger said. "Come on over here. We'll give you a treat." He led us up to the soft drink stand and asked me what I wanted. "This one's on me."

I didn't want anything, but something told me I shouldn't say no. We stood for a moment watching the big kid I'd seen before, who stood behind the counter trying to add things up and make change for a family who'd bought drinks and popcorn and animal food. He was having s slow time of it.

When they left and I'd settled on a root beer, Tiger and Priam stepped back a ways to talk, while I watched one of the spider monkeys picking lice from his partner, and pretended I wasn't paying any attention to them. I always kept my ears cocked—I've learned a few things that way.

"Be good for her—give her something to do. Instead of being a plain damned nuisance."

"Pretty young to be putting money in her hands."

"She's a whiz, I tell you. Can make change like a cash machine. And that kid you got there running things . . . not too swift up there in the cockpit. Probably stealing from you on the sly. And come September . . ."

That's how I got my first job.

"Get you used to earning your way in the world," Priam told me. "Pay for your board and keep. It's owing to me right enough—all I've had to put up with." He made a face like he had an ache with nothing to cure it, and I went off to work the picture puzzle the social worker gave me before she moved away.

I was good at fishing the sodas out from the ice chest and filling the little packets of bread crumbs and bags of limp lettuce and vegetable tops and fruit Tiger collected free from the groceries to sell to folks that wanted to feed the animals. And I was good at making change. I got to keep two dollars of it every week after Priam took his cut. I put it in a little purse I had to keep it from the camp and hid it down near the arroyo under a special rock.

Things were pretty busy that summer. People pulling in to see the jungle at their doorstep. And since it was hot and dusty, they bought lots of sodas. I liked talking to people and hearing where they came from, and I'd look at the kids and try to imagine how it was to go traveling with moms with lipstick on and shiny purses and tall, good-looking dads, mostly with nice teeth, and friendly smiles and cameras hanging around their necks.

When nobody was around, I'd go visit the animals because neither of us had anything much to do. And Ralph would tell me stories about them. He'd worked a lot with elephants and big cats, and he'd take me on his rounds and tell me about his days traveling with a circus.

"That's really exciting," I said, ready to be excited just about anything.

"It's an interesting life," he said. "I liked being around the animals, especially the elephants. You get close to them. And I sure didn't like the way they were treated. They can be awful cruel in the way they train animals in some of those big circuses. The trainers showing off for the public." He let me take that in.

Of course I'd never seen a circus and it sounded like a whole other world. It sounded like something magical.

"Animals have a lot to offer," he said. "If you listen they'll tell you things. I swear it." I was ready to try for it.

Sometimes he was all jittery, complaining about Tiger and the zoo setup. Too crowded. And Tiger was skimping on the food. "Those guys—I don't understand them. Why aren't they in real estate? They don't know what the hell they're doing. You think they care anything about what's sitting inside those cages?"

I tried to keep my eyes open to see how the animals were doing. The little tiger always looked glad to see me. They didn't have regular names—just a label like Bengal Tiger with a piece of Latin underneath. I tried to get to know the animals. I started talking to them, and it seemed like they were listening. Sometimes I'd sit real still and go over a bunch of names in my mind and see what came to me. Then I'd try out different names on them. Gave me something to think about. I could tell the big male tiger liked Caruso, even though I tried Hercules and Elvis.

It took a long time to get to know about the kit. Ralph liked to wrestle with her, just play with her like any cat. And he let me play with her too. I loved her. But mostly she was in her own space and a lot of the time seemed to be thinking or dreaming. At first I thought she was like a fairy princess who'd been stolen away from her land and home and turned into a tiger that had to wander for years till she was rescued from the wicked magician who'd betrayed her.

But then Ralph told me she came from somebody's apartment, where she sometimes slept in her owner's bed. It seemed more like she'd forgotten how to be a tiger, Ralph said. He didn't approve of keeping wild animals for pets. "Wild animals ought to be wild," he said.

I called her Antoinette.

"That's just right," Ralph told me. "She's lively and lovely—and that's what it sounds like. They need names—lets them know who they are." Then he muttered to himself. "Which is a hell of a lot more than some people know."

Antoinette liked it when I played with her. Ralph gave her a stuffed owl to bat around. She lay on her back, holding it in her paws, and raked it with her hind feet. "Disemboweling her prey," Ralph said. I knew what he meant. The owl didn't last long. He put in a couple of cardboard boxes and she had great fun leaping into them and sitting there like she'd found her spot. Sometimes he'd put a collar on her and take her out for a walk on a leash. He'd let me hold onto it. He made me be real careful—didn't want me taken by surprise or getting clawed or bit.

"They don't mean to be rough, but they got claws and teeth. They're still wild animals. They're ruthless, cats are, even the domestic ones. I figure they're thinking all the time about the bird or the mouse they're going to catch. Only that's not all of it," he went on. "They can be affectionate too. And everything they do is beautiful. Just watch how they move, how they sleep—in curves. All of them. Beauty and grace and playfulness—all of it together make them what they are—cat." He looked

48

at me. "Yes. Cat. Think of that."

It really struck me, what he said, like he'd put something in front of me that was missing from my life and that I'd have to discover. Even though I couldn't really speak to it or know what it meant, I did try to be on the lookout for it. Even in our old tomcat, Hank—what he was.

The tigers were a big draw at the zoo, but it must have been hard just lying around with nothing to do except let people gawk at them. I could at least roam around a bit.

Ralph kept saying, "I got to get out of this place." I could see how it was getting to him, seeing the way things were going. I couldn't think of anything to say that would help matters.

On the animal side the camel was maybe doing the best, though I knew his legs were bothering him from arthritis, just like Priam's, and he was feeling droopy and irritable. He'd sit for long hours in the sun with his legs folded under him. I came up close just once and he gave me a look as if to say, "Don't even bother." He looked like he was going to spit. Ralph never let the kids on his back—just on the burro and the Shetland—and that was a good thing.

In the afternoon the yard was blazing hot. No shade to move to. The sheds weren't much better. And even the projecting roof boards of the stalls didn't help much. The animals just kept pacing till they'd had enough. Then they flopped down and shut their eyes and slept and kept on sleeping.

They didn't eat much either. Most of the stuff Tiger collected from restaurants and groceries wasn't healthy food for them. Fit for the crows, and Ralph would throw half the stuff away. Then one morning, when Ralph gave Tiger a piece of his mind, the two of them started yelling at one another, and the way Tiger was waving his fist, I was afraid they were going to duke it out. But suddenly Ralph got all quiet, kind of dangerous-looking, and turned and stalked off.

"Asshole," he muttered, and shot Tiger a nasty look over his shoulder. He didn't show up for a couple of days, and I worried about him. Tiger went around swearing and cussing, he had to do all the work himself—even had me running around.

49

He jumped all over Ralph when he finally turned up. "Where the hell have you been? Are you working here or not? I oughta fire you."

"Just go right ahead," Ralph challenged him. "What'll you do then? I'm only here on account of the animals."

"What d'you mean? I've given you a chance . . . Who else would give you a job?" Tiger backed off.

But Ralph went dark and angry and just glared at me and wouldn't answer when I spoke to him. I had to work to keep back the tears.

Then he came to himself when he saw my face and told me he was sorry. He grabbed me up in a hug. "Oh, I'm so sorry, Sweetheart. Do forgive me. It isn't anything you've done. Just me and my bad mood." Then he hugged me again. "You're my best girl—always." Then I couldn't hold back.

Because I had to do something, I took some of my money and bought hamburger to give to Antoinette and Caruso. Then because it wasn't fair to the others, I saved up and bought enough cheap hamburger to give all the cats and dogs a treat. The meat they were getting wasn't all that much and not all that good. A lot of chicken near the end of its career and scraps of beef or pork the butcher had trimmed away—some of it starting to smell. Caruso would sniff it and stand there of two minds. If he was hungry enough he'd eat it. He was getting thin. Sometimes he'd sit and pull out pieces of his fur.

"You're too beautiful to do that," I told him. "Please listen."

"It's a crying shame," Ralph said. "He earns a living off their backs and he treats them like dirt. All cooped up in that little space. At least give them a good feed. Give 'em good meat and plenty of it. Horsemeat to fatten them up. Ever hear a big tiger purr? Like a motorboat." I wanted to hear that.

The animals took hold of me. I knew how unhappy they were. I couldn't stop thinking about them. I carried them on my shoulders like a weight of bricks. They padded into my dreams and roared and bellowed. They scratched and bit and clawed each other. Their fierceness was sharp as hot needles that drove into their own hides. I could hardly stand it.

"The animals are getting sick," I told Priam.

50

"Well, Miss Smartie Pants, they oughta put you in charge, you know so much."

What can I do? I asked them.

Set us free, they pleaded. Their cages were all locked up. But just suppose they were let out. What would happen then? They seemed to sink back deeper into their bodies as though they wanted to forget they were alive. The dingo, coyote, and fox were so thin you could count their ribs. By the end of the summer, the parrots had plucked out so many feathers they looked scruffy as old carpet and sat on their perches like they'd been stuffed. All their spirit had leaked away into the air—whatever they had of beauty and grace.

Tiger himself seemed to be losing his grip. You'd see him one moment and then he'd disappear, taking off in the middle of the afternoon, leaving everything to Ralph and me. He wouldn't show up till after Ralph closed the place up for the day. Then he'd slouch in to count up "the proceeds," as he called them, add up every dime, frown as he paid us once a week, put the rest in his wallet, and march off. Some days he looked at us like we were to blame for the thin pickings. Maybe he thought we were stealing.

One afternoon when nobody was around, I found Ralph among the reptiles, taking the python out of his tank. He put it around his shoulders and let it crawl down his chest. I sucked in my breath. I could hardly stand to watch. I wasn't sure what to think about that.

"You want to try?"

I wasn't sure, but something in me wanted to do it.

"I don't know," I said. "It looks creepy." When I was little, a centipede came crawling up my leg once when I was in bed. I screamed like something was about to kill me. But now with the snake, something in me wanted to try. I stood debating.

"I bet you don't scare easy," he said. "You can do it. You don't want to startle them. They got to trust you."

I wasn't sure—I wanted not to be afraid.

I had to look around inside for a quiet spot. I took a couple of deep breaths, then Ralph lifted the snake up to my shoulders, and it came on around. It was an odd feeling at first, something like that crawling

51

on me. It wasn't slimy at all, rather silky in fact. At first I held still as a tree trunk. Then I held out my arm and the python came down my arm and around my waist. I was tingling all over, and I felt happy too. Ralph grinned at me. It was like I'd passed some kind of test.

"You like that, huh? They don't take much bother, but you got to keep them the right temperature. Neither cook them or let them freeze."

I was hardly listening. I was replaying all the sensations, knowing there was fear still there, a dark place beyond anything I knew. And something else—different, but I couldn't say what it was.

It seemed like Ralph's mood had changed, as though he was trying to give me the best of himself. I spent time with him whenever I could, helping him feed and water the animals, so I could hear his stories.

The last one he told me lay closest to his heart—about the one circus he loved, where he handled a half-grown elephant named Tillie. "Came to us as an orphan right out of Africa. Poachers shot her mother. She grew up with me. We loved each other. She'd curl her trunk around me, give me a hug."

A small outfit in Missouri with only one ring—"A glorious circus," he told me, as he described the acrobats, the Cossack riders and their feats of horsemanship, the Flying Wonders on the high wire, the jugglers and clowns, and Lola, who rode the elephant. A whole parade leapt up before my eyes. It was like I was there. And the more he described, the more I wanted to be in their midst.

"Color and lights and music," he said. "Skill and daring. Think of putting yourself out there—taking the risks in spite of all the dangers—plus bad days and small audiences . . ."

I'd never seen him so excited. His eyes lit up. His forehead glowed. Even his bald spot gave off a special shine.

"They were the best—one big family," he said.

"Why did you leave?"

"Like I told you," he said, "it was a small outfit. They did things on a shoestring. Then too much competition—TV, films, sports. They had ten good years. And those were the best of my life."

After that I never heard Ralph complain. He just kept things to himself and did his rounds like a robot. He got a bad cough, bronchitis, and was gone for more than a week. I really worried about him and about the animals. Tiger again had all the work to do himself. He needed help, especially with the cats, and brought in some guy, Eddie, who acted like the whole place was a bad scene and quit after three days.

Tiger had a distracted look. Now there were times when he let the water bowls go foul or empty and I'd drag out the hose and try to get water to the animals. It was hard work. Since he knew I was doing it, he just let everything drop into my hands.

The animals kept visiting me at night—pacing up and down. *This is a prison,* Caruso groaned. *We're dying here.* In my dream I did my best to comfort them. *When I grow up, I'll bring you all home and give you good food, and there'll be lots of room where you can run and be free.* It was no use. *We are dying into our freedom.* I'd wake up breathless and scared, but I didn't know what to do. Once I sat up yelling. The animals were lying all around me in scraps and pieces. I could hardly recognize them.

"Some of the animals aren't doing well," I said to Tiger.

"They think they got privileges," he snapped. "Full of themselves—that's what, just because they perform for the public. Never saw an animal yet that didn't want to up its standard of living." He strode off, muttering. "They think they got troubles."

One of the troubles he probably wasn't expecting was a big dark-haired woman who pulled in one afternoon and stood over me like a tower, then spoke out in a deep voice that had no nonsense in it. "What are you doing here, child, and who runs this outfit?"

I could hardly find my voice. "Mr. Tiger Higgins."

"And where is this Tiger person?"

"I believe he went into town, ma'am."

"And left you here by yourself? Outrageous." She wrote something in a notebook she was carrying.

Since school was in full swing and hardly anybody was coming in, Tiger left me in charge when he went off in the afternoons. Ralph came in when he felt up to it, but he wasn't working whole days. Often Tiger brought back the smell of where he'd been, and I didn't want to get near him.

"Just tell anybody looking for me that your dad's gone to town for supplies," he told me, "and he'll be back in a jiffy."

I didn't want to tell that kind of lie. And I couldn't have told it to her. She didn't offer to buy a ticket but started walking around among the cages, inspecting the place and writing things down. "And what's your name, honey?" she said, when she came back.

I didn't want to tell her everybody called me Missy, even when I'd gone to school. And I'd left behind my paper name that nobody ever used. Something struck me though. I had named the tigers and the other animals, all except the python—I wasn't sure about him yet—why couldn't I name myself? I could call myself anything I wanted. It struck just then what exactly I did want.

"Grace," I said. Just pulled it out of the air. "My name's Grace." And even as I said it, I knew it was a secret thing, and I'd be telling it only at the right moment.

"It's a good name," she said, looking me over. She started to say something, then just muttered, "the jackass." She put a card down on the counter and said, "Give this to your Mr. Tiger." Then she put away her notebook. "Well, darling," she said, smiling a little, "with a name like that I'll bet you'll break out of whatever cage you happen to land in. Just you remember that." Then she was gone.

I spent the rest of the afternoon mooning and dreaming, trying to figure out what she meant. When Tiger turned up two hours later, wobbling as usual, he glanced around and said, "Not much business, huh? How come you didn't sweep up?" He jerked a thumb towards where the brooms were kept.

"My job's behind the counter," I said and went back to the magazine I'd been studying.

"Oh shit," he said, and walked away.

The Dream Seekers

Part I.
The Seekers

There it stood all in sunlit glory, lost in the radiance of itself: towers roofs casements doorways, intersecting planes of white and dazzle: the Seventh City. Beneath, the lavender glow of bluffs, sun reflected, from which the city seemed to float, dissolve into luminous turquoise unmixed with cloud. And beyond, the peak enclosed by mist, Mt. Xibalba, home of the gods. Merely to look brought pain-the leap of joy and longing beyond the ache in his bones, from the night, the many nights on hard ground. The white radiance washed over him like water. Filled him, floated his heart into his eye, turned him, the Kid, into his gaze and lost him there. Sucked down all that had threatened to swamp him: days and years of useless wandering to reach this pinnacle. Nights of confusion and dismay, falling about in drunken stupor. Not caring where he threw his carcass or what squalor choked his mind, what voices lacerated his ear. Truculent voices, ringed with cigarette smoke and raucous laughter insisting the bouts he staggered in were the true delights of the flesh. And they were-for they took him beyond it. Took him past his anguish, only to land him in a swamp. Then the voices in his head took over, denying the existence of any city except the mean streets where he was being dragged to the end of his tether. Only some obscure impulse kept up the maddening itch. Drove him insane beyond all knowing why.

He was staggered by the shining spectacle, barely able to stand, like the survivor of some fever, still subject to its attacks. Let him hold the City in his eye; let it not be a mirage. To look back now was to fall into the running rivers of self-loathing.

"Well, there it is," Mordecai said. As though it were a fact to be reconciled—with what? A stoop-shouldered comment from one who'd sweated his way to arrival and had to be convinced it was worth the trouble. The tone beneath the words suggested he'd seen it all before. Seen everything, had had his nose rubbed in it. Had reached no point of rescue. "God, my aching bones. And it's damned hot ." He mopped his forehead, hunched his shoulders, stretched his arms, as though he'd just stepped into his body and found it too tight a fit. "Maybe I just sweat more these days."

The Kid refused to look at him, as he grudgingly acknowledged what he owed him—his life: kit and caboodle, the whole miserable bundle. To make matters worse, it was a debt he could see no way of repaying.

"Never have made it without you, Mordecai," he forced himself. "Thanks for taking me on, seeing things through." He tried for a tone to cover hypocrisy, smear the honey over intention: to dump him, get rid of him, the lumpish presence. The old long-suffering look. He, the Kid, had to be alone to meet his bliss. To experience it in its incandescence. Even from this perspective, the city, Tiranya, promised more than the Kid could have imagined. He chafed to plunge into its gleaming appearance, wander its streets, discover its temples and palaces, turn his eye into sunken gardens, let his spirit rise into the play of fountains. But Mordecai gave no sign of shoving off.

"We're not there yet," Mordecai reminded him, in his infuriating way.

Even though they'd met with mischance the night before, it hadn't occurred to the Kid to harbor misgivings as they reached the end of their trek, though oddly familiar noises began to break through the natural sounds he could expect—cock crow and donkey bray. For some days they'd hiked through a stretch remote and barren, with only an occasional hamlet inhabited by the indigenous people, where you thought no one could live, a few scrawny sheep or goats dotting the cactus-studded landscape. Occasionally in that nowhere, they'd come upon a campesino on donkey or mule, making his way through the

56

hills on some narrow footpath towards an unknown destination; then as they'd come forward they found a house of adobe and wattles with a broken-down bus parked in front, though how it managed to get there in one piece over rocks and ruts and what it connected with was unclear. But now as they moved through the last cut in the hill and descended, there it was:

"Jesus!" A road, if you could call it that. More an obstacle course, narrow, not built for traffic, blacktop rutted, washed into the road bed in spots, but now hustling with bulldozers and cement-mixing machines, a crew of workers engaged, while a thin stream of traffic worked through barricades and detours.

"My God," Mordecai said, as they left the path and descended to the level of the cars. "Where does it all come from? The last time I saw this place it was stagnating in its own backwaters."

The Kid was dumbstruck. It had been all so clear to him; he'd rehearsed it till it was more real than anything else he harbored: a city, hardly more than a village, isolated, lost in transcendent reverie, given to the murmuring spell of litany and ritual, while sun and moon illuminated a life that kept its simple, heroic patterns. Only now a red sports car crawled up, followed by a utility van and something fancy, a Cadillac maybe, dust on the fenders, bumping slowly along the overburdened road. They caught sight of tour buses bearing down.

Mordecai paused once more to take in the city. "The old home town," he said. "A sight for the blind." He did a little soft shoe routine, as he crooked up his neck. "Oh, but there you are," he said, gesturing to the sun. "Ready to brighten everything into the latest nutty idea. Great, huh?"

The Kid, disoriented, let it go. They were at road level now. The tour buses passed him, jolting the travelers. The Hallelujah Discoverers Tour. Eager sharp-voiced female with microphone doing a background information prep. "The Lost City of Lemuria," he caught. Two other buses drew up: The New Age Symposium. The Flowers of Syncretism. Youth and gray-heads, limp from travel, were sucking at their water bottles, hanging out the windows, fanning themselves with brochures.

57

What had happened to the air conditioning?

"You know, I can hardly remember what it looked like when I left," Mordecai went on. Am I out of it or what?" He touched his forehead. "From here it looks the same. Hello, old beauty—if that's what you were." He hadn't made any move from the puzzle of mixed feelings. "But God, will you look at the goddam cars. And tour buses coming here?"

"I see them, so fuck it," the Kid said. His nerves were raw from lack of sleep, as well as from his keyed-up expectations. He had a sudden vision of hell as they walked single file along the virtually non-existent shoulder: being mired in disillusionment with only Mordecai's voice droning in his ear. What if they were stuck with each other, could neither part company or keep from driving each other nuts. He was almost frantic.

"Just look over there," Mordecai said, moving down from a little bridge they'd reached. "The river's dry as bone. Looks like they haven't had any rain for a decade. It figures. They were cutting off the timber when I was a kid. Probably still are. Look at those hills—hardly a goddamned tree. I was noticing that when we were coming down. Little scrub cedars creeping along the ground. Erosion— Dried up the clouds from down below. The rain just quit coming. That's what I heard." He turned. "So what do you think of that?"

A fly buzzing in his ear. How could he think? The traffic was at a halt now. A woman had emerged from her car to see what was ahead. "We're almost there honeybun," she assured the little kid strapped into her car seat in the back. Almost where? Here was the source and measure of all irony—that he would have twisted his brain, heart, liver, lights, loins—whatever to find a place already known to the whole world. A secret only for him. How had he managed to screw himself up so high? By making for himself a little specially cultivated garden spot with one small pond that only he could gaze in. And that was all he'd been able to see—the image in his head and how he'd find his way to it, dump the past and live. The great explorer. He was ready to gnash his teeth.

"You're full of it, you old fart."

"Why, what did I do?" Mordecai held out his hands, palms open. "You think I'm just talking. Okay, so I talk–an old habit. Sometimes my left hand talks to my right hand and sometimes my right hand to my left hand. Sometimes my gut talks to my prick and sometimes–"

"Lay off–"

"Okay, okay. Just filling up the space."

The Kid paused again. He turned away from the road toward the city. It was there, somehow real, beyond vocabulary. What syllable could meet the long anguish of his desire? Okay, so everybody was beating the track to get there. Maybe they were all in the same boat. To each his own, maybe. Somehow he had to hold on–right now there was nothing else. "Just look," he said, in spite of himself. "Doesn't it take your breath away?"

"Yeah–" Mordecai also paused. "–so long as I don't choke. You gotta be careful, kiddo. Perfection is heady stuff."

"Damn you– You're a prick–"

"For every bubble." He grinned. "A good place for a prick." "What are you complaining? We're making our way. Careful there, that bastard's trying to pull out at that flat spot, God knows why. They don't believe in shoulders in this part of the world."

"I've got eyes–you don't have to look out for me."

"Something to do in my old age. Don't get me wrong, Kid. I love this place, you wouldn't know how much."

From Mordecai it was sloppy sentiment. "I can take care of myself."

Mordecai, the fly. His laugh alone could send you into a complete funk. The Kid struggled to hold onto his one overwhelming impression, the gleaming city, before doubt cast a stone, sent everything flying. What he'd sought for so long, what he'd hungered and thirsted for beyond food and drink, he now had to cling to in the face of all distraction. It was his last chance, or so he told himself. He was almost twenty-eight and had nothing to show for it. Now all or nothing–it had come to that.

"No pal, you don't need me. Hell, I know that–even if I'm your

59

so-called angel in distress. Look, just look at me." He stood there, arms open, as though it was his distress he was offering.

More than he could bear–as though he were being offered the chance to join his to Mordecai's.

"Have I ever given you a bum steer–in all the time you've known me?"

He snorted. "Two weeks? Is that a lifetime?"

"Could have been."

The Kid pulled away and strode off. "Don't rub it in."

"Okay, sorry." Mordecai dashed up in front of him, held out his face. "Here– Hit me in the puss if I ever mention it again. Look at me." He held open his palms, first one, then the other, as though shaking them out: See, no guile, not a thing up the sleeve.

"Get lost, will you. I don't need this." It blocked his path, this sagging bulk, clothes rumpled and clammy looking. No telling what he himself looked like, after two nights wrestling with mattresses in cheap hotels, followed by their endless nights on the ground. At least he'd been able to hold onto his anticipation and the freshness of sleeping out of doors under the stars.

Until the previous night–throw that into the can. Awakened as he was by a flashlight beam in his face, three unshaven faces behind it, hands with guns. Though he knew some Spanish, he didn't understand much of their lingo–enough to know that whatever the bastards wanted, they had no compunction about killing the pair of them to get it. One of the guys was pawing through the little bag with his gear, then shoving his magician's hat rakishly on his head, holding up Billy's cape–velvet with silk lining, his mantle of inheritance. The Kid was more appalled by this sacrilege than by the threat of their demise. Though he was ready to jump the guy, he held back. No point getting both of them killed. The punks cleaned the money from their wallets and tossed them aside. What next? Maybe they wanted to kill them anyway. Mordecai kept trying to put in a word here and there, but was cut off each time with a snarl. The Kid had looked from one face to the other in the uncertain light, trying to read their prospects.

60

"Holy commerce and confusion," Mordecai said. "Will you look at the tour buses, for crying out loud. They've got it all timed. Get here during the prime time, so everybody can trip over each other."

The Kid went into a violent fit of sneezing from the dust kicking up around him. After he'd recovered, he kept up a sullen silence. The news wasn't good and Mordecai was probably reveling in it, Jew that he was. That's what they did–they had a whole history to beat their breasts about. And what made that so special? As if Mordecai had anything to offer, knocking about, being knocked from there to here–son of the Wandering Jew. The Kid could tell him a few things himself. And this was his home town? What was a Jew doing there in the first place? As if he'd ever had a home. What had chased him out of this candidate for Paradise?–if that's what it was. Mordecai's curse? Not just to wander, but to be jaded beyond a jaundiced eye. Coming back with an eye filmed with prior disillusionment–when all the Kid wanted was a little clarity.

Another piece of IRONY. The glue of his existence. What had been waiting for him in his quest was Mordecai. Mordecai blundering into the same bar in Ventura City where he happened to be pulling off a few card tricks, passing the hat. How come this sorry specimen, for whom even home was no place to go, this Mordecai (number one) had any kind of taste for magic and (number two) was going the same place he was: Tiranya, my town, my place of origin? My God, I'm headed back there. Why don't we make it a team. Worse luck. It didn't sweeten his mood to acknowledge that he owed everything to Mordecai's help. He hated himself for that.

The Kid paused to sneeze again, came up for air and looked into the singular landscape of Mordecai's face, as he piled up the gezuntheits, its divers tracks and erosions, like the desert they'd been traveling through. What had drawn down the loops of flesh under the eyes, sunk in the curves down from the nose, left its tracks along the brow? What fate? If he stuck with him, he'd probably find out, get the whole story– and who needed it? He'd been in too many bars already. Reached the bottom of the Sad Story bin, the dumpster of dumpsters. He could add a few chapters of his own to the rubbish heap-the one he still could hardly think about-the death of Billy, who'd taught him everything. And then Grace, his sister, all the family he'd had—just disappearing. That wasn't all. He wanted another story. Wouldn't even mind reinventing the past—something beyond the dust bin or the loony bin. So, Mordecai—

Only the nose remained stalwart—a monument that still held the territory despite all. It carried the whole history of the race. All in a nose. You could see someone had busted him one, shifted the monument, left a crook before the descent to dark caves. The nostrils could have given passage to an army. The rest betrayed him: lips soft as a woman's, waiting for some as yet undiscovered sensuousness. And the eyes—open as a wound. A fringe of gray hair around a mottled dome tied up the works, bundled its offerings, as the face conceded everything that had happened and then some. Made apology for being alive.

The Kid made a quick turn back to the City, as though, if he looked away too long it would disappear. The traffic was moving through the maze of road building equipment, a worker ahead with a sign that alternately said slow or stop. He could hardly see what lay ahead. That too he had to face on top of everything. The last night had almost anni-hilated him. No telling what would have happened if, in the middle of their palaver, Mordecai hadn't recognized the *jefe* of the trio. Boyhood friends. They fell into each other's arms. It required only sworn oaths of friendship and loyalty, Mordecai's watch—a present from old Putzer, the rabbi, he told him later—and all their money to get them out. They were the wrong game, Mordecai explained to him later— The banditos had their sights on a real estate developer a taxi driver was supposed to dump off at the right spot. Even so, the two of them had been lucky to get off with their skins. One of the crew wanted his hat and cape. "He's a magician," Mordecai protested. "He's gotta have the tools of the trade." "*Para la Fiesta*," the *Jefe* interceded. With a look of disdain, his cohort threw down the hat and cape. Maybe they'd have done something for the guy's image, the Kid thought.

"Don't let it get you, Kid," Mordecai had tried to assure him as they stumbled on in the dark. "They're nature lovers, just trying to live off the fat of the land."

"I thought I'd left them behind in the inner city peddling dope."

"Probably do a little of that too."

He couldn't let this faze him. At least they were alive, free. The city was indeed there, and he couldn't let go of a certain stubborn hope.

He'd been sure he was on to something when he was bumming around in Mexico. Figure it out. Now he saw a car with Florida license plates, another from New York, even one from Quebec. So there must be fifty thousand brochures out there. For him only, it now appeared, the search had been a navigation toward a mystery. People he'd talked to had led him into ambiguities instead of sending him to a travel agent. Maybe they couldn't understand his clumsy efforts at Spanish. Or perhaps they'd responded not to what was there, but to what he dreamt of.

"*Amigo*," they said, "what you're looking for doesn't exist. There was a town like that once, but it got cut off a hundred years ago. And you know what happens." He didn't know, didn't want to guess. He felt a brief flurry of excitement when he heard an old man speak of a village high in the mountains he had known in his boyhood. "You have to go on foot or by mule," he told him, "And they don't take to strangers. A friend of his, *un amigo de corazon*, had gone there and been run off with knives. He couldn't even remember the name of the town. They spoke a strange language—not even the indigenes could understand it, his informant told him. A couple of parrots had been captured who spoke that language to each other, but no one could understand it. When one of them died, the mate let out a series of squawks and curses the owner had written down, but which still remained to be deciphered by scholars. Like the Mayan hieroglyphs?

Surrounded by rumor, conjecture, legend, fantasy and stretchers, the Kid was unable to cut through to the facts. What was the Seventh City, if indeed it existed? No one he spoke to had actually been there. Maybe the city, remote, sealed in isolation, had kept itself mysterious by design. The name could have been changed. Maybe it was guarded from outside, by indifference or envy. Since the Seven Cities Territory didn't belong to Mexico or the U.S., but lay between, in such a tangle of legal confusion both countries had insured their domestic peace by ignoring its existence. All the more reason to go there.

Unexpectedly, he'd had a stroke of luck. Digging into the corners of the Governor's library in the basement of a neglected archives in Ventura City, he'd come upon a hand-written leather-bound volume by a certain Stanley Billings, Esq., chronicling his travels to the Seventh City of Cibola during the years 1890–93. His heart leapt. The introduction indicated that the writer was an Englishman who'd traveled extensively in the Caribbean and Mexico before venturing into the Seven Cities Territory. The Kid had sat bemused for hours in the dusty archives reading descriptions of a flourishing city. The writer had stayed long enough to learn the old language that some still spoke and be introduced to various customs and ceremonies. Hints of enthusiasm were not quite muffled by the aims of an exalted prose. Esoteric practices. Forms of magic. Magic!—to bring things back to life. He read the way a dog hunts out a bone, the promise of revelation frequently ending in blurred ink. Unfortunately the outer edge of the text had, at some point, been damaged by water. He made leaps of guesswork and surmise, ending in complete frustration. The text left off abruptly without conclusion. What had happened to the writer? How had his journal landed in the archives? Questions to toss in with the others.

At least he found out there was a Seventh City. On his first visit to the Territories, he'd been told with absolute conviction there were only six. Now he learned Tiranya was oldest of the Seven Cities, with a culture going back to the dawn of history. That appealed to him. Part of an ancient confederation united in trade and cultural pursuits, it had, during a period of civic chaos in which two brothers fought for the leadership, either taken itself out of the group or else been set adrift—it was not clear which. In any event, it had controlled what became the Seven Cities Territory. As the other cities were being established, it took ascendancy over the whole area. In it even now, the writer asserted, at the time he was writing, could be found the remains of an extraordinary culture.

Its development had been interrupted a second time when the

64

Spaniards came to Mexico during the Conquest in the Fifteenth and Sixteenth Centuries, Tiranya had been given to the rule of a member of the Spanish nobility, a certain Duke of the Carbayhal family, along with a large tract of land. Even so, the city flourished, as a number of families settled there, some among Carbayhal's relatives as well. The writer emphasized another period of high culture, a flowering of learning and the arts, drawing a small but advanced group of thinkers, as well as artists from outside. But less than a decade later, the nobleman had been seized by the Inquisition for heresy and burned at the stake. A period of chaos followed, during which a certain sacred talisman disappeared, the culture consequently weakened by the loss of its symbolic power. So far nothing the Kid couldn't have found anywhere—the city had had its ups and downs. He read on.

Much of the next period, the inhabitants spent resisting the Spaniards and the power of the Church. The city had been in constant quarrel with the Territorial government. Meanwhile the other cities had thrown off the city's influence and gone their way. Remote, hard to supply, the Spaniards found it difficult to maintain a garrison there—it was all but abandoned. Ultimately it refused to submit to outside jurisdiction and dropped all reference to itself as The Seventh City. So, the Kid thought. That explains it—why there were only six. Known only as Tiranya, no longer part of the configuration, gradually the city had subsided into oblivion.

He sat with that statement awhile. Forgotten by the outside world—what had happened to the rituals and magic? Clearly, they hadn't been lost. An enthusiasm worked through the stilted prose. The writer had witnessed certain practices closely guarded by a small coterie that kept alive esoteric knowledge. How far back it went could only be imagined. To the Olmecs, and Mayas, Billings concluded, and to other indigenous peoples who had come subsequently. All mingling with the cultural influences brought in from outside. "And imagine," he wrote, "that I have been among those rare and lucky few to witness the Ceremony of the Twins and The Flight of the Serpent." Maddeningly, he had refused to describe them. The Kid wanted to kick him. "But the most thrilling of all," he wrote, "is the unfolding of the Night Bazaar." Whether he'd actually visited it was unclear.

The Kid saw himself looking through a window he had no clue for entering. There followed an example of a sacred text, and the Kid scanned its pattern of symbols, drawn to a language he couldn't understand but that evoked a sense of age and time, of things held precious and lost. One thing was clear: Billings had gone where few others had ventured and come away with an experience the Kid desperately wanted for himself. Beyond all doubt Tiranya had been a hidden Paradise.

One moment his labors catapulted him to the height of enthusiasm, the next, dumped him into the pit of despair. His mind was a jumble: he didn't know what he knew or didn't know. It had been a century since the traveler visited the city. Did it still exist? In the book, a rough hand-drawn map located the city in the mountains, but when he consulted a recent map, though he could find the general area, no such town was indicated. All the more reason to see for himself.

Once the city had everything to offer. Who knew what might still be there? As a kind of talisman for his journey, he stole the book, as though having it in his possession might solve its riddles and answer his questions. Any city that had survived so long must have preserved somewhere in its cellars a few secrets—if only it might be the knowledge to end the chaos in which he swam. The idea struck him that he should put the book under his pillow. Soak it up while he slept. A mistake. Mornings when he woke he felt as though he hadn't slept at all, but had spent the whole night wrestling giant lizards or stranger creatures, now animal now human, that eluded him in shapes of smoke and twisted laughter. Other nights he waited in a run-down restaurant where no food had been cooked and the stove in the kitchen sat cold and empty. Or he entered rooms where he was bossed about by cockatoos, flamingos, and myna birds whose shrill voices sent him running to fetch biscuit peelers, hop scotches, tray trimmers, and square needles, and screeched with laughter when he returned empty-handed. The book teased at him and tore his heart, possessing him even when he was awake. He was going mad. At times he wanted to destroy the book and blow himself out like a light—find some peace, even if it had to be in oblivion.

From the hills above, the city still beckoned. He could see where a narrow road wound upward. A new fear struck at him. Suppose there was really nothing there. A mirage. What had passed through time might leave nothing more than a thin stain on the present. A small figure of panic shivered and snatched at straws of conviction. But then, what the hell—what did he have to lose? When had he had anything he wasn't more than willing to toss into the trash? Except for that brief period with the Carnival for the Gods, when, together with Grace, they suddenly had a place of their own. Before then, when they'd been living with the old man who cursed and beat him—he still didn't know who he was exactly—he'd been hardly more than an animal, unkempt, running wild, never in school, while Grace was off working to support them. He thought of how odd it was to be with people, the way he'd followed Billy around, not even sure he wanted to take the next step. He wouldn't talk, but kept silent out of a sort of canny instinctiveness to avoid being held accountable. But Billy drew him—seemed to have such a large investment in being human, even if he was only a handyman who did a few tricks, the Kid strung along. "Illusion," Billy'd say. "Now you see it, now you don't. You never know but what it turns on you, into something real."

What was real was Billy's magic, some force of his own that kept things together. The way he looked out at things and let them be what they were. Billy had brought him to speech out of his hostile silence, had taken him beyond the first syllables, of rage, of hatred of the world. Drawn him toward some dawning possibility he might grow up into. Until that terrible moment— He tried to blank it out, but it haunted him—the night in Old Town at the height of their perfomance when the fire broke out. He could still smell the burning wood, hear the cries of panic as the crowd rushed out. And afterwards, Billy collapsing on the ground outside, having been struck by one of Grace's snakes in his effort to rescue her. Snakes with poison in their fangs. Where was your magic then, Billy? And he was left only with Billy's cape to take back into his rage and grief.

"God, I'm hungry," Mordecai interrupted him "I could sure use something to fill the old gut. Once we get up the hill there's somebody I can get hold of who'll give us a meal, a place to flop down—or at least know where to send us. Those guys who held us up gave me a pretty good rundown. Count your blessings. Good grief," he said, looking around.

If anything, there was more confusion than ever. After the tour buses had pulled off into the spaces allotted to them, the cars directed to the parking lots, a throng of people were now on foot toward a cluster of buildings. Apparently this was the first step, except for some few who could climb directly into taxis.

Hungry, exhausted, light-headed, anguished and inspired, the Kid was hardly paying attention. They had passed several gas stations and motels and were now approaching a series of stalls and shops. From all sides they were accosted by vendors holding out shawls, and post cards, wooden toys, and bottled soft drinks. "Hey, Mister. Good prices. I sell cheap." Waylaid, trying to run the gauntlet, they found it almost as difficult to get past the vendors as to keep a place in the crowd. From the food stands came odors of frying meat and chili that made their stomachs churn. Ahead was a large building that looked to have some official function. People began forming various lines.

"None of this was here before," Mordecai said, bewildered. "Cafes, bars, tourist shops. Looks like it was thrown up in the middle of the night. Look way out there, will you? I think they're putting in an airport. Jeez, what are they coming here for?"

The Kid was mortified.

"Boy oh boy, am I hungry," Mordecai reiterated. "My stomach's about to digest itself. Moses and monotheism, I'm hungry. It's that damned Fernando heisting all our cash. You can hear my guts growl."

"Cut it out."

"All right," he said. "Kick me if I do it again."

"You don't think it's a temptation?"

"Look, there's a tourist office. I gotta see what's going on. You want to come in with me?"

"I'll wait here outside," the Kid said. While Mordecai went in, he leaned against the wall of the building, watching people go by. A couple with a small boy, trying to eat ice cream cones before they melted. A gaggle of youths carrying backpacks, talking, laughing, in spite of the heat. He was beginning to get restless. For a few moments the street was empty. Then a group of retirees being herded along by their leaders. Nearly all with cameras around their necks; some with video cameras filming their way along. His attention shifted to a mongrel with a torn ear going cross-grained through a forest of feet, getting shoved from here to there. "Damned mutt almost made me trip," a heavy-set woman complained. "I think it's a good thing we got here before the Festival," her companion said, as she stopped and put a hand out to the dog, "Hello, little fellow—" Festival—the Kid remembered now that one of the bandidos had made some reference to it. "Don't touch him," the heavy-set woman said. "Those strays carry all kinds of diseases."

Who did I think I was? the Kid accused himself. Another Stanley Billings—walking there in his shoes? To come upon a little closely hidden valley with noble savages, who'd throw open their arms, teach him their native tongue, reveal all their mysteries, make him into some kind of shaman and marry him off to the local princess. What blinders he'd put over his eyes. He wanted to throw up. Whole throngs had beaten the track before him—now they goddam had to pave it, fly airplanes in. And was everybody like him—blinkered by their own fantasies? Thinking they'd walk out with a story all their own?

"We have to go this way," Mordecai said, now at his side. He looked sour.

"So what did you find out? They moved back into the crowd.

Mordecai shook his head. "The news isn't good. There's all sorts of rigmarole, passes and what not. I couldn't make it out. They either don't know anything in there or have a grudge about telling you anything. Like they're doing you a big favor. They were out of maps too. So now we go up here, on the left side. That was the one thing she made clear. The others go on the right. Thank God those guys left us our

69

passports—they can sell them, you know."

They were approaching the building indicated and could see now that the road was closed off apparently to all but taxis and approved vehicles. Most of the tourists distributed themselves in various lines marked by a green light above. Mordecai and the Kid entered a line on the left. "None of this were here before either," Mordecai said. "You didn't have to do anything special to go up to the village. More goddam bureaucracy. Lines and waiting." Only their line moved slowly. Apparently it dealt with special cases. They waited as the man in front delivered a long explanation in Spanish and a whole sheaf of papers. Ultimately he was turned away; something was missing. Mordecai looked worried.

"What's the problem?" the Kid demanded.

"It's so damned complicated I can't make it out," Mordecai said, troubled. "Seems like he's got the wrong stamp on some documents."

Mordecai took out his passport as their turn came up and presented it to a heavy-set official inside a little windowed cubicle, his name tag identifying him as "Sonny" Gonzales.

He looked at Mordecai with aggravated patience and handed it back. "This got you across the border. Now let's see your papers."

"Papers? What papers?" Mordecai said. "We're here to visit the city. Myself I'm coming back."

"You're a resident?"

"Used to be," Mordecai said. "It's my home."

"Then you have your current status papers. Otherwise you have your business papers. If you're a tourist, you have tourist papers. If you aren't any of these, you get walking papers. Sabe?"

"I've inherited property here. I'm a resident."

"Look, I haven't got all day. You got your papers or don't you?"

"What d'you mean papers? I grew up here. I lived in a house—I had an address."

"How long since you've been here?"

"Twenty-seven years ..."

Gonzales laughed in his face. "The world, *señor*—have you been living in it? Don't you recognize the present government? I need to see your papers."

"I've got property—an inheritance ..." Mordecai insisted.

"That remains to be seen." He was fiddling with his official stamp. "Legally," he said, "foreigners don't own property here. It must be you don't know that."

When Mordecai started to protest, Gonzales interrupted him. "Yes, foreigner. *Estraneros*. You have relinquished the right to live here. You have to apply to the office of *El Presidente* six months before your intended arrival and be given approval. Average waiting period is six months, sometimes longer—in special cases."

"What?" Mordecai objected. "My aunt lived her for seventy-seven years. And seven months and seven hours—" he went on, all worked up. "I'm her nephew. I went to school here, I was confirmed here. I was a boy here, I was—"

"Stand aside," the official said. "You're holding things up. To the Kid. "You have papers or don't you?"

They'd hit a dead end. The Kid held up his book. "How about explorer papers?"

"A wise guy, huh." The official rose from his chair.

"Look," Mordecai said. "We're dead tired, we've been on the road for days. We need to get to the hill. We have friends there. We've got to talk to somebody."

"Who do you think you're talking to?"

"We've got to see your boss, your supervisor."

"That depends."

The man behind them, in business suit, shirt and tie that held up even in the heat, with briefcase in hand, had been shifting about with mounting impatience, glancing every other minute at his watch. The Kid felt his breath on his neck. They were holding him up chafing at the starting gate, keeping him from the race. The Kid saw a greyhound with a rabbit in front of him. No, not a rabbit—a moving dollar sign. He was groomed for the competition. Not an ounce of fat on him. Lean as

71

a chisel. Blue eyes under sand-colored eyebrows narrowed on the goal. He cleared his throat. "This delay is inexcusable," he said. "I have business here—official business."

Gonzales waved the two of them aside like moths, disdain flipping over immediately into apology. "Terrible to keep you waiting, Señor Trowbridge. Do forgive. Welcome back, sir." To Mordecai and the Kid he said curtly, "Wait in there," indicating the brick building that stood on the other side of the passageway.

A faint hope stirred, but for what? The Kid stood rooted to the spot, till Trowbridge shoved him out of the way, moved up and presented his papers.

"What are we waiting for?" Mordecai demanded.

The guard shrugged. "Wait or don't wait—it's up to you." To Trowbridge, he said with exaggerated deference. "It's been a while since we've seen you, *señor.*"

Mordecai still lingered, a question half formed. The Kid was too weary to think.

"You know the company—send me traveling all over. Just got back from Montevideo." The phrases came chopped out like messages thrown from a train. He was in motion even as he stood.

"You're not a man to pin down," Gonzales said, with a little laugh. "Me, I haven't budged." He stroked a small mustache.

A bottom-line man, shaped for Frequent Flyer Miles. If you added them up, the Kid thought, he'd probably spent a full twenty years in the business class, lap-top going, cellular phone at his ear, not even noticing the gin and tonics he sloshed down. The other had been measured by his cubicle. Even Gonzales' head looked flattened. His life was in his ink pad and stamps.

"I get to dream of all those exotic places," Gonzales said, ingratiating. His dream—while the Kid had been dreaming of this place.

"I hardly see most of them," Trowbridge said. "In—do the business—get on with the next thing."

A little smirk of acknowledgment: the man was a marvel. "You've requested six months this time, I see." The tone was questioning.

"It's been approved," Trowbridge said casually. "Got my clearance in two months."

"For a six months stay?" Gonzales said, impressed, acknowledging connections well beyond his level or ken. Still he didn't appear to be in any hurry to stamp the documents. He turned slowly through the pages, found a place at the center that particularly interested him, extracted an envelope, opened it, nodded with satisfaction, stamped the documents several times with force and conviction, gave Trowbridge a fulsome smile and gave him a card.

"They're sending someone for you," Gonzales said, to take you up to the *Casa de Huespedes*."

"Wait a minute—I have reservations at the hotel," Trowbridge said.

"The *Presidente* has arranged matters," Gonzales said. "Just present the card to the driver—" He pointed. "—over there."

Mordecai gave the Kid a significant look. "Come on," he said, motioning him into the waiting room, "I think I get the picture."

"What do you think'll happen now?" the Kid said.

"Nothing much," Mordecai said, "unless we can put our hands on an engraved portrait of Ulysses S. Grant."

The Kid looked at him.

"I mean money talks. And Jackson is a piker. Papers, my ass."

The waiting room was bare and comfortless, except for two rows of connected wooden seats with metal arms, some of which were broken and a large new-looking soft drink machine that hummed in the corner. Its glare illuminated the room more emphatically than the blinking fluorescent light overhead. Outside was the dazzle of sunlight, but inside the timeless night of bus stations and hospital waiting rooms. A bulletin board mounted on one wall offered official notices and announcements of city activities. Above it, making his presence known, was a large framed photograph of a figure in military dress holding a riding crop, his chest strung with decorations. Underneath, block letters: "El Presidente, Ramon Callegos." The Kid examined a square-built figure with a beefy face, a pair of small eyes keeping watch above a carefully

73

trimmed mustache, prissy mouth, cleft chin. Mordecai looked closely. "The new kingpin," he said. "Like a brick shit house." He studied the picture for a long moment. "He doesn't have the macaw or the sun sign," he said. "I guess it figures."

"What's that?"

"The symbols of leadership," he said. "Light and knowledge."

"Who is the guy anyway?"

"Military take-over to bring the government back to the people—that's what they all say. The *Principe* never had his picture anywhere. That was the old days. Before the new regime. I could never get the whole picture. Gallegos, eh? His show all right." Mordecai reached in his pocket for one of his cigars. He drew out the packet, mournfully examined a couple that had been bent, the outer leaf broken. "They left me my cigars," he said, looking over the wreckage. "But then the bastards had their own cigarettes. Probably don't allow smoking in here either." He hauled over a waste basket at the side of the soft drink machine. They sat in silence while Mordecai made a ritual of his cigar. He salvaged the longer stub of one, and searched in his pocket till he found a bent paper clip, nicked the end, reached in for a book of matches, made several passes with the flame, questioned the way the cigar drew, jabbed a couple of times with the paper clip, and finally satisfied, drew in a puff. His mood improved. The Kid got up to study the announcements on the bulletin board.

An hour later, they were still no wiser. "It's hotter in here than it is outside," Mordecai said, "—if that's possible."

The Kid felt his arms trickling with sweat. He leaned back, stretched out his legs, examined the fly specks on the light fixture, then got up, went over and jiggled the return button of the soft drink machine. No luck. He took a turn around the room again. Stifling, the air; flies cruising—a sour smell of waiting and boredom. It irked him to have his discomfort reflected from Mordecai's sweating face. It only made him want to jab at him, say something nasty and wounding. Fortunately, a brief commotion outside distracted him. Escalating voices, a round of accusations. At least someone else was having a bad time.

74

"Don't you threaten me, you dirty bastard. I know you."

A little piss and vinegar. The Kid moved toward the door to see what was up. He caught the back of a colorful outfit fanned by long black hair. High cheek bones—when the woman turned. "You won't get a bribe out of me," she yelled. "I know your lousy game."

Then she flew into the room like an exotic bird—orange, lavender, green. She was splendid and silvery—silver earrings dangled from her ears, silver leaves adorned her neck, a silver concha belt clasped a narrow waist. A source, too, not just of color, but fire. She hit the Kid like a comet, and he wanted to take in every bit of her. The black hair that gave off a kind of coppery light as it flowed down her back. The high cheekbones that created little shadows. Her wide mouth and full lips. She was stunning all right. But it was her eyes, large and dark, that took him past appearances and promised depths and challenges he could only guess at.

The air crackled when she spoke. "I'll not bribe them," she said in his direction, as though to make him an ally. "I'll wait the bastards out. Irregularity my ass— The fuckers." She moved away and dropped into the seat across from Mordecai. She was still steaming. "They'd find irregularities in the papers of Jesus Christ."

The Kid waited a moment, then ambled over and sat down next to Mordecai.

Mordecai laughed ruefully. "So how much do you have to slip them?

"Routinely fifty dollars American money. More for special favors. If they tried for more than a hundred, the higher ups would be down on their necks. But I won't do it." She shook her fist.

"With us it's not an option," Mordecai said.

"You got any money at all?" the Kid asked uselessly, glancing at the coke machine. "I've got about thirty cents."

"Not a centavo." Mordecai reached back for his wallet, opened it up as if to see if some miracle had occurred. "Nothing. Nil. Nada."

"Maybe you should just have let them knock me off," the Kid said, just to be saying something. He glanced over at the young woman, who sat clenching and unclenching her fist, absorbed in her fuming. He wanted her attention.

"What are you saying?" This time Mordecai was offended. "They'd have taken all the loot anyway. They like to think it was a transaction. I know those guys—"

"I thought you were big buddies."

"Yeah, they'd weep at my funeral—if they bothered to come." Mordecai shrugged. "Don't worry, those types are always around—hibernating under the rug. They just need a little encouragement."

"Yeah."

"What happened?" the young woman said, interested.

"We got robbed," the Kid told her. "Looks like you have to work past the banditos to get here and then after they strip you find some way to bribe your way past the gates."

"They should have better planning—let each bastard take his cut." Mordecai mopped his forehead, shifted his bulk, crossed his legs and uncrossed them. No more good out of his cigar. He examined the nubbin regretfully and let it fall into the wastebasket. "Looks like we'll have to apply other strategies as they say."

She looked at them questioningly. "They took all your cash before you got here?"

"They were out for bigger fish. We stumbled across their path."

She got up suddenly, went to the coke machine and put in some change. She pressed several tabs before a can came hurtling down. She put in more change, brought the drinks and handed one to each.

"How kind," Mordecai said. "God, I'm dying of thirst." He and the Kid broke open the cans, poured the liquid down their throats.

"I'm Aurelia," she said, and gave both her hand. The Kid let go reluctantly. After they'd introduced themselves, the Kid wanted only to keep up the conversation.

She looked them over, must have seen two unlikely companions. "What made you come here?"

"My aunt died. She had a property—a house that's mine now."

"Well, good luck," she said.

76

The Kid was hard put for an answer, but before Mordecai could push on to elaborate, the Kid said, "What about you?"

"I grew up here too, but I've been away—" She sighed. "My father wanted me to go out into the world." She said this as though this had been a dubious undertaking, then added. "To go out, he said, so that I could come back—to give time for something to open. But now—" she shook her head.

"Then you know the city," Mordecai said.

She shrugged, as though this too were in question. "I knew it once. It was the air I breathed. But what city have I come back to?"

"I know I've been gone a long time, but all this is unrecognizable." Mordecai said. "The bureaucracy! And the tourists! Thick as fleas. What's the deal?"

Aurelia gave a little snort. "They're looking for some miracle here that's going to change their lives. Who knows—maybe there was something once. The old ways that lasted—for a few poor Indians that weren't killed off. Only now it's a big deal. People come flocking. They come here to gawk and flash their cameras. They think that's what it takes." She let go of her anger, then went on, remembering. "I don't know—it was just what I grew up with, lived with everyday. Then when I was a kid, a handful of artists came to paint here because they loved the light. They lived with families here. There was only a posada or two for travelers."

"There was nothing—I mean nothing—here while I was growing up," Mordecai said. "A few Mexicans, Indians, craftsmen. What do I know? My aunt kept a tight rein—maybe she knew something. School, a couple of friends. She sent me away when I got restless."

"People started coming—maybe fifteen years ago now. The word got out: here was Paradise—unspoiled. Now everybody's looking for a week or two in Paradise. After the takeover, the developers smelled money."

"This little isolated spot," Mordecai marvelled. "Hardly a dot on the map. It's like I've died and come back to Ventura City."

"You'll see all the hotels on the outer edge—I went through the tour books. Plunge pools for every room, though the rest of the city is dry as a bone." Her anger flared again. "It's a crime against the spirits," she said. "Earth—water. They'll take their revenge, believe me."

Spirits? Did she really believe in them? It wasn't the place—but the Kid was burning to ask.

"They've hit the big bucks, eh?"

"What Gallegos has stashed away would take care of a whole population. So my friends tell me. He and his cronies have got a finger in every pie. A bunch of crooks—that's all they are."

The Kid couldn't take any more. At that moment only Aurelia's presence kept him from rushing out. "How long do you think they'll make us sit here?"

"What we need right now is a crying baby," Aurelia said. "Or a hysterical five-year-old, saying 'Mommy, please, I'm hungry.' That usually speeds things up."

"I could have a shot at it," Mordecai said. "Boy am I hungry," he intoned. "Hey, you out there—want to hear my guts growl? Boy oh boy am I hungry." The Kid gritted his teeth. "Boy am I—"

"Okay—we get the point."

"Otherwise we could sit here till the shift changes at midnight. By then they'll get tired of you. Maybe it's different with me."

"But then will they just send us packing?" the Kid said.

"Don't worry," she said. "They don't want to hurt the tourist trade with something ugly. It's not to their advantage," she assured them. "Nor to make trouble for me—at least not yet. I see through their tired trick to get me here."

She was gutsy. She had the goods. Whatever the obstacles she'd put up a fight. The Kid couldn't get enough of her.

"No," she said gently, as if she were still answering some objection. "This is where I belong."

"What brought you back?" he asked in a low voice, afraid he might push her away with a question.

"Betrayal," she said with such bitterness he flinched. She paused for a moment, then reached into her purse and drew out a piece torn

78

from a newspaper. "See this," she said, handing it to him. "It's my father."

The Kid saw the picture of an old man whose eyes he immediately recognized. They were hers, keenly intelligent and yet so warmly accepting you were drawn immediately, but with a quality that perhaps age and some greater knowledge had imparted. He wanted to stand under their gaze, to have them look deeply into him and tell him what was wanted.

"I would like to know him," the Kid said.

"Yes," Aurelia said, "even if he weren't my father, I would call him a great man. That's why it's so—" she couldn't find the word. "It's beyond outrage— They've charged him with being an offense to the city. For the past three years he's been under house arrest." Tears burned in her eyes.

"But why?"

"They invent things. There doesn't have to be anything behind it. It's because he's what he is—and they're what they are. You try to live out the dream of what your life should be—and somehow you're a threat. Then suddenly you're in a nightmare."

The dream of what your life should be. She'd hit him where he lived. Wasn't that just it—something that lay under all the scabs and scars and wouldn't be put down? It had to be there, or else why the impulse that worked through him but somehow lay beyond him and left him in continual torment? If only someone could lead him to what he was. For starters, he burned to shove everything aside and join her in her anger. Leap into some cause, some fight against the nightmare that kept taking various shapes.

"Only now," —her voice fell to a whisper— "they say he's dead."

"You mean they've done him in?" Mordecai said.

"Not exactly—I believe he's still alive. That's what I've come to find out."

Before she could say more, a stranger broke into their midst. His hand flew out to compensate for some deformity that twisted his hip or leg and gave a rocking motion to his body. Not only out of balance, he was entirely out of his element, dressed as though for some role in a play not yet written. Tight black pants and white shirt with ruffled front and embroidered sleeves; embroidered silk vest. Rings glittered from the hand that went flying out, and a diamond sparkled from one nostril. His expression on first looking around the room was as though he'd been hit by a bad smell. Then he saw who he was looking for. "Aurelia love," he exclaimed. "Oh, just look at you sitting here in this awful place. How long have you been waiting? I'm so sorry about the misunderstanding."

Surprised, she stood up. "Jaime," she said. "What are you doing here?" She acquiesced as he gave her a peck on the cheek.

"Serving the public," he said with the suggestion of a bow.

"Tender little reunion," Mordecai muttered. "He doesn't care how long we've been cooling our heels."

"Yeah," the Kid said.

"What's this about my father? What have they done to him? I must see him."

"Hold on, hold on. All in good time."

"Jaime, it's an outrage, I tell you. What do they think they're doing? An offense to the city. Its—"

"Calm down," he said, his voice soft as feathers. "I'll do whatever I can in my official capacity—"

"And what's that?" she said sharply.

"You don't know?" He seemed as much surprised as offended. "I'm in charge of Hospitality."

Oh, great, the Kid thought. The welcoming committee.

"Oh— Congratulations."

"The *Presidente*—" he gave the title full force and reverence— "absolutely depends on me. He has me in every morning to ask my advice—" He let the news sink in. "But particularly now when the Fiesta is about to begin. It's gotten to be a big thing." He inclined his head, as though to suggest something of where the credit was due. "You're welcome here."

"Like a toad," Mordecai muttered under his breath. "The Big

80

Man."

"We'll take you to the *Casa de Huespedes* where you can spend the night, courtesy of the city—until your clearance is verified."

"If I can't go to my father, I'd rather be in a hotel," Aurelia said, "—if you don't mind."

"You won't find a room in the city," Jaime said, as though it were his triumph, but with an insistence that would brook no argument. "We're already booked up till the end of the season. We can't build the facilities fast enough. But you'll be comfortable, I assure you. We're set up just for occasions like this—and for special visitors."

"These are my friends," Aurelia said, gesturing toward Mordecai and the Kid. "They can't get in. Official rigmarole and bullshit. They've been robbed as well."

With a flick of the wrist, he waved away all obstacles. "Not to worry. Any friends of yours ... You have only to come to my car outside."

"Anywhere's better than here," Mordecai said, as he stood up and worked the kinks out of his muscles. "My back's killing me. Those seats aren't made for human anatomy."

"I thought it was your gut," the Kid said.

"Yeah, well—name your torture. It's up for grabs which'll do me in first."

Grateful, they moved outside where the afternoon dazzle blinded them. "I feel like I'm walking out of a bad movie," Mordecai said, as they walked toward the parking lots. A couple of buses were filling with visitors to take them up to the city. Jaime led them to a white Chrysler parked in a place designated Official Use Only. He opened the doors and motioned them in, indicating the front seat for Aurelia.

"Hey, pretty fancy," Mordecai said as he climbed into the leather upholstered back seat with the Kid. "My Uncle Howard used to drive one of these—before he landed in the slammer."

No one commented.

"Air conditioning," Mordecai said, when they were under way.

"What a relief. I can't remember heat like this here. But then the whole climate's changed too."

"They don't want cars up in the city—except for taxis and official vehicles," Jaime explained as he passed one of the lumbering buses. "Everybody else rides one of those."

"How privileged we are," Aurelia said.

As they wound up the hill, Jaime brought up their various links to the past. Did she remember so-and-so, from the time they were in school together? He filled her in on various careers. Aurelia, however, was not to be distracted. "What has happened in this city?" she demanded. "Everywhere I look there are these hideous new buildings."

"A lot of changes," Jaime said. "A lot of improvements. The *Presidente* has virtually eliminated poverty—singlehandedly. It's a miracle. There are clinics here now, brand new schools for the children. We've become modern."

"I don't remember being poor," Aurelia said. "Maybe too many people are rich."

"And people are safe here. Except for a few minor problems— you know, an occasional pickpocket, the inevitable domestic brawl—you won't find any crime inside this city."

"Good news for the bandidos," Mordecai said. "They've got a monopoly outside. Where did all these hotels come from?"

"More tourists every year," Jaime said. "See that one going up over there? Fifty million for fifty rooms. Imagine, a million dollars a room."

"They paper the rooms with gold leaf?" Mordecai wanted to know. "Make the plumbing out of 14 karat?"

"The designer comes from San Francisco," Jaime informed them.

The Kid sank down in the seat and stared straight ahead. At first, Mordecai was completely disoriented. But once they got past the hotels on the outskirts of the city, he gave the Kid a poke, "Hey, look at this, will you. Now it's getting familiar." He became animated as he pointed out various landmarks. "The Old Palace, see. Not too much different. The square—only, my God, what have they done? Shops everywhere. Everything under the sun." Then again as they wound through the streets, he couldn't remember where he was. When they paused before a white wall, with a courtyard partially revealed by an iron gate at the end of a passage, he was stunned.

"What's this?" Mordecai said. "How did you know? Why are we stopping here?"

"What do you mean, *Señor*? This is where you'll spend the night." Jaime rang the bell.

"What d'you mean what d'you mean? It's my house," Mordecai said, as the maid opened the gate. "My inheritance. What I came back to claim."

Down to Earth

(A Book of Improvisations)

The Kid wanted to do something for me—and the question was, would I let him? He's on his way up in the world these days, and there's no telling how high he'll soar. I figure he's got the goods, but when I put my mind around what he's aiming to do, my breath catches. Really what Dusty struggled to do on the grand scale: take the world by the tail and change things at the core. It takes a kind of high-feathered ambition all right—to think you're the one who's going to make a difference. On the outside it looks like arrogance And it takes a powerful imagination. Sometimes I can't help thinking it's an affliction, when the idea gets to buzzing your brain worse than any horse fly, and keeps biting at your rear when you're not looking. I watched Dusty take his knocks, let me tell you, thinking he could create some kind of grand celebration at the heart of the city, carnival and circus all rolled into one. And all it finally added up to was one rag-tag little outfit you could never tell would make it from one day to the next.

What the Kid has done is put together a circus that sends your heart soaring and keeps your blood tingling. I've seen it. You just never want the show to quit—one great act after another, full of rip and daring, and comic routines to double you over. Something to celebrate all right. And I keep thinking—imagine, there must be something to it after all, the way it lightens your foot, puts a glow around the edges of the day. It would be enough to gladden Dusty's heart to have an heir to carry on his dream. That way—if only he could know about it—he could maybe think it wasn't all for nothing. But then the Kid knows magic, what it's supposed to do—the way it can change you, even if the world gets caught in the same old snags.

I'd sat with his letter a month or two—time is pretty sluggish down here in the Retirement Belt—one flawless day floating up on top the other. The light comes up gradually, bleaching away the dark, as though to save you from the shock of a new day, time passing—time running out. Then when you're free of all surprise, the sun tilts up from the horizon, a red ball into a net of cloud, setting its glow on the day. Breeze warm and wet and salty as a lover's smooch while the folks up north are shivering in their longjohns and digging out their cars. Oh, we have our moments, enough to scare the socks off the citrus growers. But mostly you sit with a glass of something inspiring, waiting for a pelican to sail over and fling itself down tail feathers over wing—tip into the waves for his fish, or else for the resident egret who makes the rounds to mooch a few shrimp. Knows a good thing when he sees it. Expensive tastes. But then I've never known a creature that didn't want to improve its standard of living, up its bracket, so to speak.

Hadn't been able to lift a pen to reply. Had hardly done a thing the past year or so. Hard to think of a new life when the old one is shot to hell. Even when you spend a good many hours wishing it all had been different. Dusty gone—a hard going. Everyone I'd known scattered to the four winds. And what was I any more? An old piece of goods marked down below cost, lying there on the shelf with the other unsalable merchandise. I'd thumbed through my fifties still flinging the old bod into a few good times, but my sixties had hit like one of those late summer hurricanes knocking out power lines and tree branches. Nothing you can get insurance for.

Then here comes somebody knocking at the door and what-do-you-know, it's the Kid himself, standing there big as life and twice as handsome, in jeans and pale blue shirt, denim jacket and sandals—looking pretty spiffy. All of it just right, like it suited him. Like he knew where he was going, maybe even how to get there. He gave me a grin and a big squeeze before I could get a greeting halfway out of my mouth. I had to keep from crying—last time I saw him was at Dusty's funeral—in the big tent. The Kid had taken care of it all. Lots of people came, even those Dusty still owed money to. And they gave him a tribute that kept me dabbing at my eyes. Spoke of all he'd aimed for, what his example meant for the circus in America, and how he'd left his imprint on the coming generation. As though you could let go all the failures, the misbegotten ventures, just forget them, and leave something shining— better than a slug's trail in the grass.

"Kid— My God—what are you doing in these parts?"

"Coming to see you—what else would I be doing?"

"I keep reading about you in The Circus Record and Spectacle," I said. "I've followed you all over the place."

"We had a great year," he said.

"And the one coming up?"

"Wonderful acts," he said. "Yeah— We're in our own place now—it'll be a challenge." I saw a little catch of hesitation in the midst of his enthusiasm. "We've got a reputation to live up to. And we've got to build on it—sky's the limit."

News to cheer me, that's for sure. "Come on inside," I said, "and have something to drink. I've got some scotch and some fixings for a pina colada." Actually I'd been itching for a little pick-me-up, though I admit it was ahead of time.

"A little early for me," he said.

"Here, there's no early or late," I said. "Time is whatever you slice it up to be. You can cut it in little squares or turn it around in circles and add a few curlicues—"

I got him settled in the visitor's chair with a glass of iced-tea, slouched down with an ankle over one knee, and as I sipped my whis-key, I took a long look at him. He'd changed—as though a certain set of qualities that at one point had been contradictory and out of balance had moved together into something you'd call maturity. Yet he hadn't gone hard or cynical. Manly—with his wavy brown hair and blue eyes and healthy skin. Good teeth to put a dazzle in his smile.

"You're opening in three or four weeks, aren't you? You got a few jitters?"

"I have no doubts about acts. And you know there'll be a few days on the edge of chaos it takes to make things come together. If Morgan delivers with the money like he's promised and keeps out of my

87

hair, we'll go great guns."

I was sure of it. I liked seeing him there. At ease, but you could still feel the energy pouring out of him. Open. None of the old suspiciousness and the big Keep Out sign. Maybe an old suffering had turned up a gleam of reconciliation, for there was a kind of humor playing around the edges. A light in the eye. If life was a joke, he was no joker. Well, it had been a long time coming. He could have gone down the tubes just as well as up the ladder, so to speak—either way, considering what happened after Billy passed on. Left a hole in his life bigger than the state of Texas. Just when the Kid had got the father he needed. After Billy left us, he went to pieces. And I won't say what I was like. Billy and I were soul mates in some fashion; it felt like half of me had been ripped out. The Kid had lost the hand that steadied him and taught him magic. And I'd lost the magic. Couldn't do a thing with him. Like trying to tame a tornado or pet a wounded tiger.

I was actually glad when the Kid cut out for god-knows-where. Pointless to try to stop him. We lost track of him—thought we'd never see hide nor hair of him. I know Dusty was relieved. Then all of a sudden he turns up, comes to see us. Had found a lost city, he told us, somewhere in the hinterlands where we'd traveled before in the Seven Cities Territory, but even more remote, or so it seemed, but "discovered," with everybody beating a path to this final, most "authentic" city. And then when you got there, a bunch of crooks and bullies. Totally corrupt. For all the phoniness, he'd had some kind of experience there that opened his eyes. He babbled on about a great love, his inspiration—Aurelia. Only she'd disappeared and he'd been trying to find her ever since. But she'd been the one to send him back to the land of the living. I had no idea what he was talking about. But she'd done him a turn—whoever she was—turned him inside out and ripped out the old lining. He was off drugs and booze, ready to find his work in the world.

Reality, he said—the old bitch. Now he was ready to face up to it, come down to earth. He got on in Las Vegas with his magic act, but he didn't like the night club scene. For a while he teamed up with a fire-eater and a sword-swallower. Did some gigs on the road with them.

Then he got into a hot little one-ring circus out of Phoenix. Became a founding partner with some fellow—forget his name, who was producer now, an old hand in the business. Had brought circus acts into his night club. Plenty of contacts, people who owed him favors. Someone to woo backers and brainstorm with the Kid about the acts they'd scouted. And the Kid was left to come up with the conception, work his ideas out with the performers, put the whole show together.

He told me about their new location—in a depressed area of the city, where they'd been given a contract to settle. The city had given them that space, along with some support, hoping the circus might bring some new life into the area, for kids and grownups alike. He hoped it would go, as well as draw people in from outside. They had to have those too. It had taken a lot of work to convince his partner. He talked about all the top-notch talent they'd gotten together—a great Cossack riding act, some hot stuff on the high wire and trapeze. I had the feeling he was trying to draw me in, although he wasn't looking at me directly. Every once in a while he'd frown as though something prickly was lying behind his eyebrows.

I was pouring myself another little booster, when he said, "I meant what I said in that letter, Alta—I want you to come along with us this season."

I suppose I should have been flattered he'd taken the trouble. "C'mon. To do what?"

"Something you'd like. Maybe wardrobe—take care of the costumes."

"Hell, I can't stand anything to do with a hot iron or a needle and thread. I did it when I had to—did a little bit of everything. But I don't come with domestic talents. Anyway, what do you want with an old bag like me?"

He frowned again. "What do you mean? Because that's your life, it's always been your life. You know it inside out, start to finish . . ."

"Just look at me, will you. You know what people come to a circus for. What would I be doing? Don't condescend."

"You think I'd do that?" the Kid said.

Well, no, I didn't.

"Besides you're getting too comfortable," he said, looking around.

I had my habits, I'll warrant. I had my platform rocker, and I spent a lot of time in it. When I wasn't out in the garden or having a drink with one of the neighbors or by myself, there was a big stack of magazines I could leaf through, courtesy of Lavinia, former queen of the liberty act, really a wonder with horses. Lived across the way. I didn't give a damn about them, the articles about 57 ways to keep your man (I'd had my innings) or forty dozen possibilities of goosing up your sex life: how to do it from a chandelier or in a diving bell; or how to fix up the tastiest dish with rutabaga or carrot tops or horses' ovaries or shrimp toes. I'd read enough about the latest cure-all, a small exotic fruit the size of raspberry from the tropical islands off Tasmania, and the seven infallible steps toward becoming a millionaire in real estate or graft. I liked the pictures. Mostly I'd drift off to some little spot-lit moment of the past. The same when I watched the game shows or the sit-coms. I'd put on my own show; the others were too dumb to watch. Time killers— and I mean, killers. Like the slow poison spiders use to kill their victims. Paralyze them first, then eat their hearts and brains.

"You want me to take on life's challenges?" I said. "Screw that, Kid—I've had my fill."

"Damn it, Alta," he said, "I want you to be part of this. Think of what you did for me."

So there was gratitude in him—I hadn't banked on it, but there it was. Mostly it should have gone to Billy, who'd taken him under his wing when he was only half a step up from being a savage. Taught him magic and transformed him. All I did was cook his meals and keep an eye on him and act like he was halfway human. Thank goodness he'd made the grade—didn't end up in jail or dead of an overdose. I don't know what you're supposed to do when somebody's got all that loose feeling playing around—he had his life now, and I had the leavings of mine.

"I want you to be part of what I've got, while I've got it." From

90

one moment to the next, I couldn't tell whether he figured it was a sure thing, or whether he was in the midst of some real uncertainty. "You need to give me a chance." He said it lightly, with a little smile. Then he added, "You could be part of the chivaree."

"What—come in with the goat?"

"You could wear any costume you like."

He knew me all right. I didn't tell him I still had two or three hanging in the closet, maybe looking for an occasion, though I hadn't found one recently. I've always liked decking myself out. Color alone can make me drunk, set me on fire.

"Who knows what you'll come up with," he said, giving me all of earth and outer space to forage in. "I want people to invent, improvise. I've got ideas in my head all right, but it takes the rest of you to make things come alive, to give them that special zing."

Oh, he'd found room for his imagination all right. I was looking at him through a haze. Hadn't given my mind to invention for quite a spell—it takes all your moxy. Then once you start, you're caught up in what lives in your head—just ripe for a pounding from outside. How could I stand it anymore? He didn't know what he was asking of me. To open up again, all the old vulnerabilities, setting up your heart for a target. And all to help him out of his gratitude. What I had was easy enough, even if you could call it a hollow blessing: not having to get up every morning wondering if we had enough to eat and to get everybody through the day or whether some sheriff was going to close us down for not having the right friends and connections or not slipping him enough bucks to make it worth his while. None of the old burdens. Feeding hungry egos, straining to see that the show held together when the old no-fail glue of ready money wasn't forthcoming. All that sweat and labor to keep the wheel on the track. All the dreams—gone now, like smoke. But that's what it is with dreams—when they vanish, they don't leave a trace.

All that effort had used me up. I'm not what I was. Even if I shed thirty pounds I still wouldn't be, though I don't feel any age in particular. Just now there's nothing pressing— The money I've got gets me by. Courtesy of a cousin who cashed it in without any other kin. (One day this lawyer turns up and says, "I've got some great news. What's the best news you could get?" "You really want to know?" I said.)

I admit I went through the family phase. Thought: here I am all alone—I'll look up a few of those kinfolks I haven't seen in years. They were nice enough—they even invited me to dinner. There was a little jittery bobbin of surprise running under the surface when I appeared—I could sense it. As though some strange creature had dropped from the sky they had to acknowledge but couldn't make any decision about, but having to take me on because I was kin.

Their furniture was worn but comfortable, having given hospitality to various kids and dogs and cats. The house was full of kids' voices and screen doors banging—the grandkids were visiting. I liked the autumn scenes on the walls and the family photographs with all the faces I didn't recognize. Family, but sure different from mine. The chicken-fried steak and carrots and peas and au gratin potatoes and strawberry-rhubarb pie were the best I'd tasted in years. Even grew their own rhubarb. They told me about the church bazaar and what their grandkids were doing in high school and college and beyond.

And then after we'd packed away her splendid meal, my cousin Ellen said, "Tell us about the circus." They were all eager. "Well," I said, "it's taken me wandering with all kinds of folks." That's all I could get out. How could I tell them what it felt like up on the trapeze, faces of the crowd just a blur below and you're flying across the tent under the hot spots. Or the way it was, all of us together for the sake of what we could do out there, as though that made us what we were. Loyalties and jealousies and sickness and dark days, just for the sake of those few moments. The craziness of it all. All my experience just shrank up into a little knot the size of a walnut. All I could say was, "Well, there was some excitement in it." Afterwards I fled back to my trailer. I just couldn't help it.

Here I don't have to talk to anybody I don't want to. Just take care of my assorted plants and Calypso, the cat, who was going to have kittens any day now. Have my early morning walk along the beach to pick up a few shells or shark's teeth, whatever the tide's tossed up. Stand there half an hour looking out over the ocean and maybe watch a shrimp boat on the horizon, knowing it's not going to move. A permanent point, for that moment anyway. Then after a few chores, a little pick-me-up. Another after lunch. Then maybe a nap. I can fill out the rest of the afternoon sipping wine and playing a little circus music, save the whiskey for later in the day after the pina coladas. These days I appreciate a little nightcap.

"Come on, Dream Girl," he said.

He could play dirty. A pang went through me. The name I went by during my glory days on the trapeze—what Billy always called me. Dream Girl. Oh, Billy—Dusty. I suppose the Kid knew what he was doing to me, tearing a huge hole in my resignation. A shark, that one. A tempter.

He wasn't a magician for nothing. He'd come down to rouse me out of my torpor, beckoning with his wand: Come, come, come, come. The Pied Piper. And already a voice struck up in the head: Go for it, Dream Girl— despite that ancient sluggish side going down to the deeps, that just wanted to drift there in the haze and vegetate. A sort of blankness. Not that I was unhappy— I was too numb for that. Or else too pickled. Nor was I at peace. Something still ached below the surface, as though all the sap hadn't hardened up yet, but still waited to be used. Despite all I could do to stifle it, something throbbed, More, more, more.

"I'll think it over," I told him. I could see disappointment congealing in his looks.

"Alta," he said, "please come. I don't even know myself why I'm asking. It's just ... I've got some kind of feeling—"

A raw note. I looked at him, trying to figure out what he was really trying to tell me. I'd been so caught up in my own confusions, it hadn't occurred to me he might be asking, reluctantly, for some kind of help. Still I couldn't make it out.

"You in some kind of trouble?"

"No, not yet. I don't know—Morgan bothers me—I don't know

quite where he's coming from. The way he talks. Now that we've had some success, I think he's got caught up by the glitz. He sees millions pouring in. Like he's some new incarnation of P.T. Barnum himself. All the big outfits—he's impressed by them. That's not where we are. We can create something, work our way into it ... make it real. But it'll take time."

"Who is this fellow?" I said, with a sudden sinking feeling. No, it couldn't be—it was a common enough name.

"Juan Pablo's his name. Descendent of the pirate—you know, Henry Morgan—that's what he claims."

"Juan Pablo!" I said. "I can't believe it."

"You know him?" the Kid said, astonished. "But I guess you know everybody."

"Yeah, yeah—way back when." I didn't want to say anything about it—it had all been so long ago. We had a history, you could say. "Used to juggle swords and daggers. He loved his costumes—all that pirate stuff. Does he still wear a mustache?" I'd lost track of him years ago. "Where'd you link up with him?"

"Las Vegas. Had a club there—did some circus acts along the way. Then after the season ended last year he turned up. He was looking for a new challenge. Liked my style."

"Well," I said, not knowing what to make of it. "Imagine him still being on the scene."

"Only—" he looked troubled. "I'm beginning to think we don't see eye to eye."

"That can be tough in this business." And the money arrangements—I didn't dare ask.

"Yeah. That's what I'm afraid of, in my worst moments. Everything sounded terrific when we first started out. Maybe I'm just jittery. It's just that everything hangs on this. I don't want to fall on my face."

"You won't," I said. "I know it. Not from what I've seen."

"The show's fine— I have confidence in it. But there's all the stuff that can get in the way—you know about that. People you were counting on—"

94

I knew all about that.

But he wasn't going to dwell on obstacles—he was all caught up. We were in a new era. The circus, the one-ring circus, was being reborn from a place where it mattered, where it reached the public in a different way from other entertainments, really drew them in, made them more than spectators. That's what they were mostly reduced to—just sitting there in front of the tv or a flick. Even sports events—there to lock. And what could be better than real skill, real daring, real danger? Being invited not just to watch, but to risk something, see things pushed to the edge. Showing people how far the magic could go. Make them take a little glow back into their lives. A change of perspective. Reminded me of Dusty all right. And the animals—he liked that connection. The comedy, too, of course. Clowns at the heart of it. The circus was going to be more important than ever—a place to explore and experiment. And dream. Oh, he had a bad case all right.

He was coming to a crossroads, I could see that. He had to make it work, he said, almost with anguish. He had to do it for her sake as much as for his own. She may have—, but she was never out of his thoughts. It was all for her now—for what she represented anyway. And what could I say for myself that would have any parallel? That it was all for Dusty or Billy or whoever—whatever they'd been striving for? I'd just leaked out into my surroundings, hadn't really kept much of anything back. As I looked at the Kid, I thought, There's still a touch of craziness in him. And it's probably catching.

So what are you going to do—sit here and wait for the final curtain? Without even putting on a show? Damn, I thought, trying to ignore whatever was playing with my head. I couldn't stand to refuse him, couldn't stand to do it to myself. "You're on," I said.

"I knew you had it in you."

I wasn't sure I could bear his triumph.

The Dream of Circus

1. Before the Show Begins

Places!

Back of the curtain what is there to see?
Elephant coming through, Yo-yo the clown
atop, careful not to bump her head
going through the arch. Babe's disappearing
tail, the little black tuft at the end. Outline
of a large presence waiting in the chute.

All the while, rings and pins leap
past the eye—jugglers practicing.
Aerialists stretching their muscles:
Sasha chalking his hands, ready
to capture Aurelia from her backward
somersault mid-air before the gasping crowd.

Mr. Bumble making faces for the baby,
the youngest star, then warming up
the violin to tickle music into laughter.
The belly dancer lighting candles
into the little flares she dances with.
The Shetland munching a carrot, the goat
with a rooster on her back.

Fragments—tricks upon the ordinary,
waiting to make a shape for wonder.

Let the horses gallop the ring; the acrobats
pile upward in pyramids, the snake
charmer, oriental, undulate the cobras—
all the glittering gestures—against gravity.
Let the clowns come tumbling in.

2. The Dance of Matter

Babe, Splendor, Theodora—graces
of the flesh. Appetite in motion,
an eye out for anything to fill
sheer bulk. Skin, cracked earth,
monumental clay.

Babe, comedienne, plays the barber,
steps on a leather strap to sharpen up

the razor, lathers up her handler's face
for a shave. Splendor raises her trunk
and leg in a pose triumphant.
The three together on their platforms
lift legs like trunks of ancient trees. These
are the motions of their public life.

But, do you know, the handler,
alone, at night after the circus crowd
departs, turns them loose
and they play tag. He slaps one
on the flank and runs, and she
lumbers after him to tag him
with her trunk. The others join
the game—three elephants
playing tag by moonlight.

3. Tiger Lily

You can't turn your back on them:
that's the first rule. They need a face
to trick them into the human sphere
for those moments in the ring among
the spectators—before they take up
the wildness that they are.

Nor can you dominate, rule with fear—
to hide your own. They know better.
Face it—they can smell you out.
To step into the cage you leave aside
the face of things—what you take
to the public—and let your thought flow
with theirs, enter the fire that shapes
the fierce tooth, stand at the boundary
where you could shed your image—it's that thin.

I've been through all those doors— Big cats:
they take the meat from my mouth,
jump through fiery hoops, but the hardest
thing is simply to have one sit patiently
on a pedestal. After the show I hug them,
listen to the engines of their purr, then up at five
to feed them their raw meat. When I take a bow,
I know what I'm bowing to—there can be no pride.

4. Mr. Bumble

I'm an old piece of work, patched
together from ill-assorted parts.
Red underwear nobody wears, striped socks,
potato nose. All the awkward gestures
and pratfalls and near calamities—these
belong to me, child of chaos.
Original offender against the social evening,
who trips against the hostess and rips apart
her dress; plays the fool where great men
cast their shadows. I play my violin
in a parody of music, repair what will
only fall to fragments. All things reduced,
taken apart to their original element:
deep from the belly's dark it comes,
snickers up the chest, tickles the throat,
exits like the original breath,
before the shaping word.
First the gods laughed.

5. Juggling Act

One, two, three—this time let's toss the pins
from hand to hand and let none drop.
Psychology is all—simple conviction.
It works. When the eye quits straining,
the pins fly of themselves, spinning up
among the lighter things: balloons, birds
in flight, clouds, planets suspended by
balancing hands.

Other days cast up
a doubt. Once I could toss eight pins,
seven in the ring. Now they clatter down—
broken birds. When Luba's dancing horse
slipped, she fell too. Three months in a cast
without work. The clown sulks
with a pain in his gut, making antic faces.
The stands are thin, the producer lies
awake. All this under the tent:
things falling—reaching for a hand.

6. On the High Wire.

Before fear
set in, across a tightrope
close to the ground
at three, she was taken by the hand—
that's how it begins, in innocence.
Then higher in the air, as balance joins
with the light sure step, and art—
to climb to the outer edge where a false move
is death, the body pushed to its limits,
the mind concentrated into a single
disk of action, under the hot spots,
above the heads of crowds, the sweat
crawling down her face. No name for
that moment a lifetime of practice reaches,
fear and daring fallen into the ease
of the foot against the taut line:
full—with the terror
of being.

7. Finale

Is it that the Flying Cranes evoke
those images of birds that tilted
across the skies of my childhood
and still speak of flight or Bracques,
whose lithographs send wings across the mind—
or the bird-man in the park who keeps
an eye on bluebirds' eggs as he
envisions a skyful of blue wings flashing?

I dream of speech with animals and birds.
I swallow the tiger's burning
with a fire-eater's plunge
and leap with the lions through flaming hoops.
The little elephant treats me to her joke:
takes the peanut with her exquisite
nose, then blows breath down the hollow
tube of trunk she steps on: a raspberry.

Clowns dancing   everywhere   acrobats
maintaining the hair's breath of balance,
jugglers triumphing over objects flying
through space and time, as they usually do

but for the illusion
of gravity.

Then just before the waking:
the figure in black, ceremonial,
bearing a white caftan approaches
the great white horse, halter dancing

with bells and red wool tufts. He leaps
over plumed tail to back, climbs the flowing mane,
stands poised on the great white head
(How does he do it?) Then the two rise
slowly into the air, while I watch
ecstatic to follow.